Love in the Time of Plague

Maximilian Krieg

Published by Maximilian Krieg, 2024.

This is a work of fiction. Similarities to real people, places, or events are entirely coincidental.

LOVE IN THE TIME OF PLAGUE

First edition. October 30, 2024.

Copyright © 2024 Maximilian Krieg.

ISBN: 979-8227026804

Written by Maximilian Krieg.

Table of Contents

Prologue: The Onset 1
Chapter 1: "Living Target" 9
Chapter 2: "Cornered" 15
Chapter 3: "The First Escape" 21
Chapter 4: "Reluctant Allies" 27
Chapter 5: "The First Loss" 33
Chapter 6: "Escape Across the Desert" 39
Chapter 7: "On the Edge of Survival" 47
Chapter 8: "Moments of Peace" 53
Chapter 9: "Betrayal in the Shadows" 59
Chapter 10: "Coming Closer" 63
Chapter 11: "False Trail" 69
Chapter 12: "Unspoken Truce" 75
Chapter 13: "Estrangement" 81
Chapter 14: "Duty vs. Desire" 85
Chapter 15: "Taken" 91
Chapter 16: "Escape Plan" 97
Chapter 17: "On the Edge" 101
Chapter 18: "Echoes of the Past" 105
Chapter 19: "Team Tensions" 109
Chapter 20: "The Point of No Return" 115
Chapter 21: "Dangerous Allies" 119
Chapter 22: "Face to Face with the Past" 125
Chapter 23: "Maze of Dangers" 129
Chapter 24: "Through Ice and Fire" 135
Chapter 25: "When It All Falls Apart" 141
Chapter 26: "The Rescue Plan" 145
Chapter 27: "Broken Chains" 149
Chapter 28: "Ghosts and Reality" 153
Chapter 29: "Face to Face with the Enemy" 159
Chapter 30: "The Flame of Hope" 165

Epilogue... 171

Prologue: The Onset

The city burned in fractured patches under a dull, crimson sky. From her lab window, Dr. Rebecca Adams could see the endless stretch of panicked traffic—cars abandoned, their hoods smashed open as though the machines themselves had given up and were howling in despair. It was no different within the sterilized walls of her lab, where chaos beat at her chest in a vicious tempo.

Rebecca leaned heavily against the cold, metal table, where rows of vials lay gleaming, a single red mark scrawled across them: *Prototype*.

"Isn't this what we wanted?" Her lab partner, Dr. Karim Jaffer, gave a rough laugh from the doorway, his voice somewhere between rage and disbelief. He looked pale beneath his protective mask, eyes blazing in a way Rebecca hadn't seen since the outbreak began. "A global crisis, the kind we get grants to speculate about, and now, what, we just pack up and *run*?"

"There's no time, Karim. This…this is bigger than anything we imagined," Rebecca's voice was barely a whisper, thick with exhaustion and terror. She closed her eyes, seeing in her mind the virus's twisted black cells, spreading under her microscope. The "Black Plague," as the world now called it, had outpaced every conceivable model.

"I'm not abandoning it, Rebecca." Karim leaned forward, his gaze flickering to the vials she was packing with shaking hands. "The vaccine is only theory. We don't even know if it's viable."

She stopped, a flicker of defiance cutting through the fear in her eyes. "I have to try. This—" she waved her hand over the vials, a grim set to her jaw "—this is more than theory now. It's the only chance anyone has left."

Karim swallowed, stepping back. "Then, for God's sake, get it out of here before *they* come."

As if on cue, the screech of metal echoed down the sterile, hollow corridor of the lab, louder than any heartbeat. A cold chill gripped her as the lights flickered, shadows sharpening. "They're here."

The infected. Another wave of those sick and twisted by the plague, drawn to the scent of fresh blood and helpless souls. Rebecca moved quickly, shoving the vials into a case, her breaths coming fast. Every second was a risk; every heartbeat felt like a countdown. She tightened the latch and grabbed the bag, her legs trembling.

Together, she and Karim raced through the halls. But the sound of scraping, inhuman groans drew closer, filling the corridors like fog creeping into every crevice. Rebecca kept her gaze focused on the path ahead, but she couldn't ignore the flash of blood on the walls, the remnants of the team that had once called this place home.

Finally, they reached the emergency exit. Karim shoved the door open, and the piercing sunlight nearly blinded her. As they stepped outside, Rebecca was hit by the stench of smoke and decay. She shielded her face as they darted past the lab's parking lot, where bodies lay discarded, vehicles abandoned.

They had only made it halfway across the lot when she heard Karim stop, his breath catching.

"Wait," he rasped. His gaze was fixed on the entrance of the facility they'd just left, where a man was stepping out, flanked by a group of followers who moved with a predatory, eerie silence. Rebecca's pulse quickened as she took in his figure, tall and imposing, with a dark coat fluttering around his legs like the wings of some cursed bird. His face was shrouded in shadow, but she could see the flash of a smile, twisted, cold.

"Who..." Karim's voice trailed off, his fingers clenching around Rebecca's wrist. "Who is that?"

Rebecca didn't know. But the sheer malevolence radiating from this figure was enough to root her to the spot. A single name echoed in whispers among the few survivors who had crossed paths with him.

Lucifer.

She had heard of him. A former tycoon, a man who had risen from the ashes of the world's collapse to lead a twisted empire. He had somehow gained control over many of the infected, twisting their minds with promises of power or salvation—or maybe it was simply fear.

As Lucifer's gaze swept over the lot, his cold eyes met Rebecca's for one brutal, soul-searing moment. His smile widened, and he nodded once, a small, mocking salute. Then he turned, disappearing into the shadows of the lab.

A shiver coursed through Rebecca as she forced herself to turn away, pulling Karim along with her. They slipped into a nearby alley, and she pressed a finger to her lips, mouthing *Silence*.

But her mind raced. If Lucifer had gained control here, that meant he was close to reaching the last surviving centers of research—the one place she hoped to reach with the vaccine.

Rebecca couldn't let herself think about what he wanted. All she knew was that if he found a way to manipulate the virus further, if he took control of it entirely, then all hope was lost. The nightmare she saw in her microscope would become reality.

The sound of Karim's heavy breathing beside her grounded her, and she took a steadying breath. "We need to keep moving. Now."

They wove through the maze of streets, the sounds of riots and screams echoing around them. There was nowhere to go that didn't reek of terror, but they moved in instinctive silence, heading toward the outskirts where she had stashed her emergency supplies. But Rebecca couldn't shake the image of Lucifer's cold, calculating gaze from her mind.

Meanwhile, across the city, in a desolate part of town that once housed luxury apartments, another figure watched the descent of humanity with a grim determination. Nolan Jarred had witnessed the end of the world more than once. The first time was overseas, in a war zone that had taken his comrades, his friends, his sense of purpose. The second time was here, at home, as he watched the virus devour the people he loved.

Now, there was nothing left for him but vengeance.

Nolan sat on the edge of a dilapidated rooftop, his rifle slung across his back, scanning the cityscape with cold, calculating eyes. He had a target, someone whose influence had spread like poison through the ranks of the infected. Lucifer. It was a name that made his blood boil, but he was disciplined enough to keep his rage under control. Rage would come later; now was the time for precision.

From the rooftop, Nolan could see the faint glow of fires across the city, hear the distant screams and cries. It was a symphony of ruin. And in the middle of it, he had one mission: find Lucifer, end him, and, if he was lucky, save what little could still be saved.

He pulled out a small, tattered photograph from his pocket, the last remnant of a life he could barely remember. A life where he had been more than just a weapon. A wife. A daughter. Both taken by the plague, and for that, the world would pay. Nolan didn't care if he had to burn it all down.

And so he watched, silent and unflinching, as the city turned to ashes.

The sky was darkening as Rebecca and Karim pushed further from the lab, weaving through abandoned streets, where buildings loomed like skeletons against the crimson-streaked horizon. Rebecca's heartbeat thrummed loudly in her ears, each beat a reminder of the vials tucked safely in her bag. She had only one purpose now: protect the vaccine. If there was any hope left, it lay in these fragile, glass-bound threads.

As they moved toward the outskirts, Karim's footsteps faltered. He paused, glancing around the empty lot they had ducked into, his face twisted in despair. "What's the point, Rebecca?" he hissed, barely loud enough for her to hear. "We're just two people. The world is...is beyond saving."

"Then go back," she snapped, her voice barely restrained, eyes fierce and unyielding. "Go back and join the rest of the damned, Karim. But I'm not done."

The silence stretched between them. Karim's face fell, his eyes dark and searching, as though hoping to find something in her that could ground him, give him purpose. But Rebecca was already ten steps ahead, her mind racing through each calculated move, each step to get the vaccine out of here.

When Karim finally caught up, there was an emptiness in his eyes, a look she knew all too well—the look of someone who had already given up. "I don't understand why you still think it's worth it," he said quietly, defeated.

Rebecca glanced at him, her lips a tight line. "Because someone has to."

In the shadow of a broken city, Lucifer watched his domain with a look of quiet, twisted satisfaction. He had seen the world transform under the weight of a virus he had helped spread, a carefully calculated act of revenge on a world that had once humiliated him, scorned his ambitions, and belittled his empire. And now, that empire had taken new form, a dark, fear-laced kingdom where loyalty was forced and obedience taken, not asked.

The infected came to him in droves, their minds dull and obedient, seeking a leader among the chaos. To them, he was salvation, a voice that promised them power and absolution. And they listened because there was no one else to believe in, no other hope that remained.

One of his lieutenants approached, a man with a scar running down his cheek like a brand of loyalty. "They've secured the perimeter around the lab, sir," he reported, his voice low and respectful.

Lucifer nodded, an idle smile curling at the corner of his mouth. "Good," he said, almost to himself. "They'll come to us. And when they do…" He let the words hang, knowing they'd carry more weight left unspoken.

There was only one way this game could end, and Lucifer was prepared to use every weapon in his arsenal to ensure it played out to his advantage. After all, he hadn't come this far, built this empire, just to watch it fall. Not without watching the world fall first.

Rebecca and Karim reached the edge of the city, moving carefully through the empty streets where the air itself felt weighted with a sickly, metallic scent. As they neared a crumbling overpass, they heard movement behind them—the unmistakable scuffle of feet on broken pavement.

"Get down!" Rebecca hissed, pulling Karim behind a car wreck. Her fingers dug into his arm as they waited, breaths shallow. The infected, likely drawn to the sound of voices, moved closer, their low growls echoing in the desolate space. She held her breath, praying the darkness would conceal them.

But then, a shrill scream broke the silence as Karim stumbled backward, knocking into a piece of broken glass. The infected froze, their eyes gleaming in the shadows as they homed in on the sound.

Rebecca's heart thundered as she pulled Karim back to his feet. "Run," she whispered, barely able to get the word out before the infected lunged toward them, their twisted forms hungry and relentless.

They tore down the street, lungs burning as they zigzagged through alleys and broken buildings, trying to shake the horde. But the infected didn't tire, their steps pounding behind them with sickening determination. Rebecca's mind raced as they neared an abandoned building, its doors partially open.

"In here!" she shouted, grabbing Karim's arm and dragging him inside. They slammed the doors shut, holding their breath as the infected scratched and clawed outside, unable to breach the barricade.

Karim slid down the wall, his chest heaving, a look of sheer terror on his face. "We can't...we can't keep this up, Rebecca," he gasped. "How...how are we supposed to survive this?"

She didn't answer, her mind focused solely on the task at hand. They had escaped, for now, but there was no telling how long their luck would last. She clutched the bag of vials tightly, her jaw set in determination.

"We survive," she said, more to herself than to him. "One way or another."

Back on his rooftop, Nolan watched the city's slow, painful descent into darkness. He'd been here, night after night, watching from the shadows as the infected tore through the streets. Every sound, every flash of violence only served to remind him of what he'd lost—of the family he could never bring back. His gaze hardened as he thought of Lucifer, the man behind it all.

Revenge was all he had left. A singular purpose in a world devoid of meaning. And he would see it through, no matter the cost.

He turned away from the edge, checking the rifle at his side. Tonight, he would start his hunt. And with any luck, it would bring him closer to the man who had stolen everything from him.

As he disappeared into the darkness, a cold resolve settled over him. In a world that had burned itself to ashes, he would be the flame that refused to die.

Chapter 1: "Living Target"

In the harsh glare of a military-grade LED, Nolan Jarred scanned the map splayed out on a makeshift command center in what had once been a sprawling mall. Rows of mannequins stared down at him from shattered shop windows, their glassy eyes still dressed in last season's trends, as though life hadn't ground to a halt a year ago. If he squinted, he could almost imagine them as his audience, gawking at the mess of tactical plans he was mentally piecing together.

Beside him, a weary-faced lieutenant tapped a finger on a particular block marked with heavy, ominous red ink: *Los Angeles Bioresearch Facility*.

"We have confirmation she's still there," the lieutenant said, glancing up with something that might have been nervous excitement—if nervous excitement were even possible in this dead-eyed world. "Dr. Rebecca Adams. She's been there for months, apparently still working on a vaccine."

Nolan's lips quirked into a dry, humorless smile. "Working on a vaccine, or holding on to one?"

The lieutenant shrugged, but his voice was edged with weary skepticism. "She's the only scientist left who hasn't gone dark, so... she's either a genius, or she's lost it like the rest of 'em." He rubbed a hand over his face, gaze going distant. "You'd be the one to find out."

"Lucky me," Nolan muttered under his breath, already calculating the best way into the facility without drawing attention—or worse, a battalion of Lucifer's infected minions. He traced a finger over the map's fine lines, mentally bookmarking points where snipers could be positioned.

The lieutenant cleared his throat, shifting his weight. "You're to bring her in, Jarred. Alive. Along with any samples of her work. High command thinks if there's anything left worth fighting for, it's what she's holed up with."

"If I find her at all." Nolan's voice was an ironic drawl, though he knew he'd find her. This sort of job—the kind that required deadly efficiency and no distractions—was his specialty. "And if Lucifer's goons don't have her first. Heard he's been sniffing around that area, too."

The lieutenant's eyes narrowed, a trace of worry slipping through his mask of composure. "You've got to get there first, Jarred. She's the last shot we've got at... well, anything that's worth a damn anymore."

"Right," Nolan said, voice laced with an irony sharp enough to cut steel. "Let's go save humanity." The lieutenant's look grew grim, but Nolan was already moving, strapping on gear and readying himself for the mission.

And in the back of his mind, something itched—the faintest sense that maybe, just maybe, this mission would turn out to be worth more than it seemed.

Rebecca Adams was standing alone in a sterile, almost too-silent lab, half-emptied vials scattered on the table before her, each one containing a carefully adjusted variant of the virus. These were hours' worth of tests, hundreds of samples that had become little more than a series of dead ends. But in her tired, desperate eyes, each failed test was just another step forward, another inch closer to saving what little was left of the world outside.

She looked up from her microscope, gaze going to the reinforced glass that made up most of the lab walls. Los Angeles sprawled beyond, a smudged landscape of skeletal buildings and abandoned streets. It was a ruined city, a landscape burned into her memory now, as familiar as the lines on her own palms. She closed her eyes, feeling the weight of exhaustion settle like iron on her shoulders.

A clatter sounded from somewhere behind her, breaking the brittle silence. Her heart lurched, and she tensed, her hand reaching for the scalpel on the edge of her desk. In the post-apocalyptic chaos, every sound carried a threat, every shadow an intruder. She couldn't afford to let her guard down, not now—not with the knowledge of the virus's latest mutation still fresh in her mind.

Mutation 417, she'd labeled it with grim irony. Just a number, a file name. And yet, it was a deadlier version, one that could outlast the original infection if released. Rebecca shuddered at the thought of the virus's relentless evolution, its ability to take whatever humanity tried to throw at it and twist itself to survive.

Adapt or die.

The infection seemed to have chosen adaptation, and with a vengeance.

A rush of footsteps echoed through the corridor outside, quick and purposeful, sending a spike of adrenaline through her. She spun around, gripping the scalpel tighter. But as the door opened, her pulse steadied; it was only Tyson, a junior researcher she'd recruited to help her.

"Dr. Adams," he gasped, visibly relieved to find her alive. His face was pale, slick with a sheen of sweat. "Dr. Adams...there's something you need to see."

She frowned, following him out of the lab and down a dimly lit corridor lined with glass cases that showcased once-valuable research equipment now covered in dust. Tyson led her to a small observation deck overlooking the main entrance of the building.

Rebecca's eyes widened as she saw a group of figures approaching, cloaked in shadow, their movements unsettlingly coordinated. The group was led by a tall man with an arrogant stride, a man she'd seen in news reports back when the world still had a semblance of normalcy—*Lucifer.*

"Damn it," she hissed, clutching the edge of the window frame. Her mind was racing. There was no way she could let them inside, not with the samples still sitting in the lab. If Lucifer got his hands on the data, on the vials...

"Close off all access points," she said, her voice low and urgent. "Now."

Tyson paled but nodded, running off to activate the security measures that would hopefully buy them time. As she watched the figures grow closer, a sense of foreboding settled over her. She wasn't sure how long they could hold Lucifer off, but she had no choice. She had to protect the vaccine—at all costs.

Outside the facility, Nolan maneuvered his way across the ruined landscape with the precision of someone who'd been doing it far too long. The shadows of the approaching night made it easier to blend in, each step calculated to avoid any noise. His objective was straightforward, though the context was less so. He had been sent to retrieve Dr. Adams, but now it looked like he was not the only one interested in her whereabouts.

Through his binoculars, he caught sight of a group moving with grim purpose toward the facility entrance. It didn't take long for him to recognize the man at the helm.

"Lucifer," he muttered to himself, a sardonic smirk curling his lips. If there was any shred of doubt that this mission was about to spiral out of control, that doubt had now left the building entirely.

Lucifer's team was equipped with state-of-the-art weapons, probably looted from abandoned military bases. If the doctor was in there, she was about to become a very popular target, and not in the friendly sense.

"Looks like I have to play the hero," he grumbled, his tone laced with bitter irony. *Get the doctor out, keep her alive, and make sure Lucifer doesn't turn her into his latest weapon*—easy enough. He shouldered his rifle, moving with quiet efficiency down toward the facility's east side, where he spotted a narrow side entrance.

Nolan worked fast, slipping through a broken window, and landing softly inside. The stale air of the facility closed around him, the silence punctuated only by the distant hum of generators. He moved quickly down a deserted corridor, his focus trained on his mission.

Rebecca moved methodically, locking down doors, checking every camera feed available on the dimly-lit control panel. The corridors of the facility flickered on the screens before her, showing nothing but vacant hallways and empty labs—until a figure moved across one of the feeds, a tall man with a determined stride and a weapon slung across his back.

Her heart skipped a beat. This man was not part of her team, not part of Lucifer's group either, from the looks of it. He seemed too... *focused*. Not mindless, not infected. She zoomed in, watching him scan his surroundings with the alertness of someone who knew how to handle himself in dangerous territory.

"Who are you?" she murmured under her breath, eyes narrowing as the figure made his way through the building with almost unnerving efficiency.

As if in answer to her question, the man paused, looking directly at the camera as though he could see her watching him. Rebecca froze, a chill sliding down her spine. She clenched her fists, torn between fear and a strange, grudging respect for his calm.

This wasn't just any ordinary trespasser.

In the hallway below, Nolan glanced up at the security camera, feeling the weight of someone's gaze on him. He allowed himself a grim smile, imagining the doctor watching him from some hidden corner, assessing him with a mixture of caution and intrigue.

Well, the feeling was mutual.

Chapter 2: "Cornered"

The air was thick with smoke, sharp and acrid, as alarms blared through the empty corridors of the bioresearch facility. Red emergency lights pulsed along the hallways, casting everything in an eerie, blood-red glow that seemed to vibrate with each blare. Somewhere nearby, metal clanged, the sound echoing off the walls in jagged bursts.

Rebecca darted through the smoke-filled lab, clutching her bag to her chest, her heart pounding. The glass vials inside clinked with each step, a reminder of the precious samples she'd risked everything to create. She made her way toward a console, fingers shaking as she punched in the security code to seal off the lab.

But her fingers froze mid-entry when a sharp noise came from the doorway behind her.

"Nice place you've got here," a voice drawled, dripping with ironic charm.

Rebecca spun around, her gaze landing on a tall figure silhouetted in the doorway, the red emergency light catching on the edges of his rough features. He looked like he'd stepped right out of a post-apocalyptic action film—dark, muscular, and armed, with a rifle slung across his back and an expression halfway between boredom and exasperation.

"And you are...?" she managed, her voice steady despite the alarm bells hammering in her head.

He raised an eyebrow, glancing at the chaos around them. "Oh, just the guy they sent to save the woman who apparently values test tubes over survival." He gave her a look, his eyes flicking to the case in her arms. "Planning to hug those vials all the way out?"

"Excuse me?" Rebecca shot back, straightening, the indignation flaring up before she could stop it. "I don't know who you are, but this 'woman' happens to be the only person with a shot at stopping this epidemic. If you'd kindly *move*, I'll be on my way."

His expression remained unimpressed. "And here I thought scientists were supposed to be smart. That wasn't exactly a subtle entrance, lady."

"*Dr.* Adams, if you please," she corrected, ice in her tone as she swept past him toward the doorway.

He didn't move, blocking her path. "Nol—uh, *Captain* Jarred," he replied, sarcasm dripping from each word. "Nice to meet you, Doctor. Now, let's see if we can get out of here without both of us getting shot or worse."

Rebecca's jaw clenched as she looked up at him, sizing him up. She didn't appreciate the cavalier way he was handling what was, objectively, a life-or-death situation. But before she could respond, a series of sharp, metallic clinks echoed from the far end of the hallway—the unmistakable sound of someone else making their way toward them.

Nolan's entire demeanor changed in an instant. He raised a hand to silence her, the cocky grin vanishing, replaced by a sharp, calculating look. "Stay quiet," he whispered, and she had to admit the command in his voice was enough to send a chill down her spine.

Rebecca pressed herself against the wall beside him, clutching the bag close to her chest. Her eyes followed his as he scanned the hallway, his movements precise and controlled.

"They're Lucifer's men, aren't they?" she asked, her voice barely a whisper.

He didn't look at her but nodded. "The guy's real keen on making sure you don't walk out of here. Now's not the time to ask questions—just follow my lead."

Rebecca bit back a retort, though she felt her irritation spike again. She was *not* accustomed to being ordered around, particularly by a man who looked like he thought he had the world all figured out. But she forced herself to stay silent, watching as he knelt down and peered around the corner.

"Great," he muttered, a dry edge to his tone. "Looks like we've got two choices: we go down the hall, straight into their lovely welcoming committee, or we take our chances with the service tunnel." He glanced at her with a raised brow, a faintly mocking smile pulling at the corner of his mouth. "Ever crawl through a ventilation shaft, Doctor?"

Rebecca's lips tightened. "Not that I recall. But let's see if I can manage without your expert coaching."

His smile widened a fraction, though he said nothing, and instead moved to a nearby grate, prying it loose with a quick twist of his wrist. "After you," he said, motioning with an exaggerated flourish.

Rebecca ducked down, muttering something under her breath as she crawled into the cramped tunnel, feeling his presence close behind her. The space was narrow, the air thick and stale, and every movement seemed to echo ominously. She focused on breathing steadily, the scent of metal and dust filling her lungs.

After what felt like an eternity, they emerged into an empty storage room. Nolan moved first, scanning the area before gesturing for her to follow. The sound of heavy boots from the other side of the door made them both freeze, and he held a finger to his lips, his gaze sharp.

They remained still as shadows passed beneath the door, moving swiftly, determinedly. Rebecca's heart hammered, and she glanced at Nolan, who simply rolled his eyes as if to say, *Amateurs.*

When the footsteps faded, he exhaled softly. "Welcome to another day in paradise," he murmured, the sarcasm unmistakable.

Rebecca shot him a look. "I don't need a commentary on the obvious, thanks."

He smirked. "Good to know the genius doctor can see what's right in front of her. I was beginning to worry."

She huffed, irritation prickling under her skin. But as much as she hated to admit it, his competence was obvious. He moved with an efficiency she had rarely seen, a sense of purpose that seemed almost... comforting.

They navigated through a series of storage rooms, finally reaching a side exit. Nolan paused, glancing at her with a scrutinizing gaze.

"Still hugging that bag, huh?" He sounded both exasperated and vaguely amused. "Guessing whatever's in there is important enough to risk your neck?"

Rebecca's grip on the bag tightened involuntarily. "Let's just say it's not something I'm willing to let fall into the wrong hands. Especially Lucifer's."

His expression shifted, a flicker of something unreadable passing through his eyes. "Right. Well, keep close. We've got company." He jerked his chin toward the door, where muffled voices could be heard on the other side.

They slipped through another exit, making their way down a narrow corridor lined with broken pipes and dim emergency lights that barely illuminated the path. Nolan kept his pace even, but Rebecca could feel the tension radiating off him, as though he was calculating every step, every breath.

"So," he said suddenly, his voice low but carrying that familiar sarcastic edge. "Mind telling me why Lucifer's so interested in a scientist like you?"

Rebecca's gaze hardened, and she shot him a sidelong look. "Maybe he appreciates my intellect. You wouldn't understand."

Nolan snorted, though he didn't take his eyes off the path ahead. "I'm sure it's your charm, Doctor. The man does have a thing for people who enjoy working alone in locked labs."

Rebecca bristled, the urge to snap back nearly overwhelming. But she held her tongue, focusing on keeping her pace steady, her gaze sharp.

They rounded a corner, only to come face to face with a trio of armed guards, all of whom froze for a moment before raising their guns in unison.

Nolan didn't hesitate. In a swift motion, he pulled her down behind an overturned table, taking cover as the gunfire erupted, ricocheting off the walls with ear-splitting force.

"You okay?" he shouted, glancing over his shoulder at her. His face was inches from hers, his expression tense but focused.

Rebecca nodded, her own breath coming fast as she clutched the bag tightly. She felt a pang of frustration at her own helplessness; she was a scientist, not a soldier. She hadn't asked for this.

Nolan turned back to the guards, returning fire with a precision that was almost chilling. He moved with a practiced ease, his expression unreadable, his focus absolute.

When the last guard fell, silence settled over the corridor, broken only by the faint hum of the emergency lights. Nolan lowered his weapon, exhaling slowly.

"Guess I didn't have to worry about you *actually* hugging those vials, after all," he said, his voice laced with irony as he glanced at her, clearly amused by her death grip on the bag.

Rebecca straightened, her cheeks flushing slightly as she adjusted her hold. "You don't know what's at stake here, Captain Jarred."

"Oh, I think I have an idea." His eyes met hers, a flicker of something serious in their depths before he quickly masked it with another smirk. "Let's get moving before more of your fan club shows up."

She didn't argue, falling into step behind him as they continued down the corridor. Despite her irritation, she couldn't deny the faint sense of relief that came with having him beside her. She had spent so long working alone, fighting this invisible war with nothing but her research to keep her grounded.

Now, with every step that brought her closer to safety, she found herself reluctantly grateful for his presence—his sarcasm notwithstanding.

As they made their way toward the exit, she couldn't shake the feeling that this was only the beginning of something far more dangerous than she had anticipated.

Chapter 3: "The First Escape"

They had made it into the skeletal remains of what used to be a parking garage, the kind of place that once buzzed with the daily hum of commuters and honking horns. Now, it was little more than a cavern of shadows, littered with broken glass and rusted metal, its silence broken only by the distant sounds of footsteps as Lucifer's hunters prowled the area. Red emergency lights pulsed weakly from overhead, casting everything in a murky, surreal glow.

Nolan held up a hand, signaling Rebecca to stop as he edged toward the corner, his rifle raised, scanning the dimly lit path ahead. Rebecca watched him, her heartbeat pounding against her ribs. His focus was intense, his entire stance radiating a grim determination that reminded her of how alien he was to her world of labs and theories.

But as he scanned the area, Rebecca felt the itch of an idea spark in her mind—a bold, somewhat reckless idea, but one she couldn't shake.

He was distracted.

If she left now, she could slip away and get out on her own terms. *Before he inevitably dragged her into more trouble.*

As if sensing her thoughts, Nolan glanced back, his expression a mix of irritation and impatience. "You good, Doctor? Or are you going to stand there until they spot us?"

She forced a smile, one she hoped looked convincingly innocent. "I'm fine. Just trying to keep up with the constant danger and, you know, impromptu shootouts."

Nolan's eyebrow lifted, skeptical but too focused on the mission to push further. "Stick close," he ordered, moving forward again, his attention once more on the terrain ahead.

She waited until he was a few paces ahead, his back to her, and then—*this was it*. Holding her breath, Rebecca turned sharply to the left and slipped behind a concrete column, her heart hammering as she darted toward an old stairwell she'd spotted moments before. With luck, she could make it outside, get as far away as possible, and find her own way to safety. She didn't need an armed "hero" pulling her through this. Not when she had her work to protect.

The stairwell was cramped and smelled faintly of decay, but she forced herself forward, each step taking her farther away from Nolan and whatever schemes he'd dragged her into. She reached the bottom of the stairs and edged into the shadows, her bag held tightly to her chest.

Almost there. Her pulse quickened as she saw the exit sign flickering at the far end of the corridor, glowing like a beacon. Just a few more steps, and—

A low, guttural growl reverberated through the silence, freezing her in place. She turned slowly, her stomach dropping as her eyes landed on a hunched figure, its skin gray and mottled, its eyes sunken and lifeless, fixated on her with a mindless hunger.

The infected.

It wasn't alone. Shadows shifted behind it, more figures stumbling forward, their movements disjointed and jerky as they locked onto her with inhuman intensity.

Panic gripped her, hot and visceral, as the closest infected lurched toward her, its mouth opening to reveal teeth stained with blood. She backed up, her feet tangling over the debris scattered on the floor, her mind screaming at her to run, but her body frozen.

And then, without warning, a shot rang out, echoing through the corridor. The infected creature collapsed, its skull shattering in a grotesque spray of blackened blood. Rebecca whipped around to see Nolan standing there, his rifle still raised, his expression a mix of irritation and thinly veiled amusement.

"Making friends, are we?" he drawled, his tone infuriatingly casual as he stepped closer, lowering his weapon. "Thought you might be better at mingling."

She opened her mouth to reply, but words failed her. Her pride wanted to snap back, to remind him that she hadn't asked for his help, that she was perfectly capable on her own. But the reality of the situation, the memory of those lifeless eyes locking onto her, silenced any retort she could muster.

"Nothing? Really?" Nolan's smirk grew, a gleam of sarcasm in his eyes. "All that intellect, and you decide that ditching your only backup is a smart move?"

Rebecca's cheeks flushed, heat creeping up her neck. "I didn't ask for your backup."

"Clearly." He slung his rifle over his shoulder, his gaze sweeping over her with an amused scrutiny that made her feel uncomfortably exposed. "But since you seem so keen on heading right into the jaws of danger, I figured I'd stick around. Wouldn't want to lose the esteemed Dr. Adams before I can deliver you back to headquarters in one piece."

Rebecca clenched her fists, irritation flaring despite her lingering fear. "I can handle myself, you know. I didn't exactly ask for a babysitter."

Nolan chuckled, the sound low and infuriatingly self-assured. "Oh, I'm well aware. I just figured it would be a shame to let all your hard work end up as a midnight snack for one of Lucifer's pets."

The smug look on his face only made her frustration grow, and for a moment, she entertained the idea of wiping it right off his face with a well-placed punch. But she knew better. This was the man who'd saved her life—again. And as much as she hated to admit it, she couldn't deny the faint, reluctant gratitude tugging at her chest.

He was watching her, waiting, as though expecting another attempt at defiance. But the fear that had gripped her only moments before still lingered, a cold reminder of just how close she'd come to death. She forced herself to take a deep breath, gathering the remnants of her pride.

"Fine," she muttered, crossing her arms defensively. "I'll follow your lead."

His grin widened, a smug, infuriating smile that only added fuel to her simmering irritation. "Oh, well, thank you, Doctor. Glad to know you approve."

She shot him a glare, but he just shook his head, clearly amused as he gestured for her to follow him down the corridor.

They moved in silence, each step echoing off the concrete walls. Despite her lingering resentment, Rebecca couldn't shake the sense of security that came from having him nearby. His footsteps were steady, his movements precise, and she found herself grudgingly impressed by his calm in the face of danger.

"You know," Nolan said after a while, his voice breaking the silence. "If you're going to sneak off in the middle of a mission, maybe don't pick a route crawling with the infected next time. Just a thought."

She rolled her eyes, refusing to give him the satisfaction of a response. But the truth was, she couldn't shake the memory of those creatures' eyes, their lifeless, vacant stares, and the way they'd locked onto her with a hunger that felt all too predatory.

"Not so talkative now, huh?" Nolan's tone was laced with mock surprise as he glanced over his shoulder at her. "Must be a first for you."

Rebecca huffed, her frustration bubbling over. "What is it with you, Captain Jarred? Is everything a joke to you?"

He raised an eyebrow, his expression shifting from amusement to something almost serious. "A joke? No." His gaze flickered over her, a hint of something unreadable in his eyes before he looked away. "But I've found sarcasm keeps people a little saner in this nightmare. Maybe you should try it sometime."

Rebecca let out a humorless laugh. "Forgive me if I don't find the end of the world all that funny."

They fell into silence again, the tension between them thick and charged. Rebecca kept her gaze forward, focused on putting one foot in front of the other. She didn't trust him—how could she? He was a stranger, a man she'd barely met and one who seemed to take a perverse pleasure in pointing out her every flaw. But as much as she wanted to deny it, she knew she couldn't make it out of here alone.

And he had saved her. Twice now, if she counted their initial escape.

She felt the weight of the bag against her side, her precious samples nestled safely within. For a moment, a thought flashed through her mind—a strange, unsettling thought. Perhaps, just perhaps, this man could be trusted, at least for now. He was sharp, perceptive, and disturbingly efficient at keeping her alive.

They reached another stairwell, and Nolan paused, glancing back at her with a raised eyebrow. "Ready, Doctor? Or would you prefer another attempt at a solo mission?"

She shot him a look. "I'm ready."

He smirked, a flicker of approval in his eyes as he turned and led the way up the stairs. Rebecca followed, her mind whirling with a confusing mix of relief, gratitude, and resentment. She hated being dependent on anyone, least of all this man with his infuriating smugness and unrelenting sarcasm.

But for now, she had no choice. She was cornered, forced to rely on him, whether she liked it or not.

Chapter 4: "Reluctant Allies"

The night was quiet, too quiet for comfort. Outside the crumbling walls of the abandoned building they'd found, the world was cloaked in heavy silence, broken only by the faint, ominous howls of infected creatures roaming the deserted streets. In here, though, it was just the two of them—and the tension that crackled between them like an electric current.

Nolan checked the perimeter one last time before settling in beside the boarded-up window. His gaze flicked over to Rebecca, who was sitting across the room, her bag clutched tightly to her side. Even in the dim light, he could see the exhaustion etched into her features, a tension in her shoulders that didn't seem to loosen, even for a moment.

"You can relax, you know," he said, his tone a mix of dry amusement and weariness. "It's not like I'm about to steal your precious vials in the middle of the night."

Rebecca looked up, her mouth tightening into a small, annoyed smile. "You say that now, but I'd rather not wake up to find my life's work missing."

Nolan's eyebrow lifted, a smirk tugging at the corner of his mouth. "I'm flattered by the trust. Really. Warms the heart."

She let out a soft, humorless laugh, leaning back against the wall. "You don't exactly give off the 'trustworthy' vibe, Captain Jarred."

"Oh? And what vibe do I give off, exactly?" he replied, crossing his arms as he watched her, clearly amused by her response.

She tilted her head, studying him with a mix of sarcasm and something else, something a little more guarded. "The kind that says,

'I've been hired to drag you halfway across a dying country, and I'm not sure you're worth the trouble.'"

Nolan chuckled, a low sound that made her pulse jump, though she quickly brushed the sensation aside. "Not bad. But I'd add something like, 'I'll save you, but I'll complain about it the whole way.'"

Rebecca raised an eyebrow, a faint smile playing at her lips despite herself. "Oh, that's definitely coming across loud and clear."

They fell into a quiet that was oddly comfortable, the kind of silence that felt almost familiar, despite the fact that they were barely more than strangers. Outside, the distant sound of infected creatures prowling the empty streets seemed to fade into the background, leaving only the soft hum of their breathing and the occasional rustle as one of them shifted.

Rebecca glanced down at her hand, which had started to throb with a dull ache. She'd scraped it against a piece of jagged metal during their escape earlier, and though she'd ignored it at the time, the wound had started to sting, a slow, relentless burn that made her wince.

Nolan noticed her grimace, his gaze sharpening. "You're hurt," he observed, his tone neutral but direct.

"It's nothing," she replied, attempting to wave him off, but the movement only made the pain flare. She bit back a curse, pulling her hand closer to her chest.

He didn't look convinced. "Let me see," he said, his voice leaving no room for argument. He moved closer, reaching out before she had a chance to protest.

Rebecca hesitated, a prickling discomfort at the thought of letting him help her. But the pain had become impossible to ignore, and she grudgingly extended her hand, avoiding his gaze as she did so.

He took her hand carefully, his touch unexpectedly gentle as he inspected the wound. She held her breath, the warmth of his skin against hers unsettling in a way she hadn't anticipated. She glanced up, finding his face closer than she'd realized, his expression serious, focused, the usual glint of sarcasm absent from his eyes.

"This'll need to be cleaned," he murmured, his tone softer than usual. He pulled a cloth from his bag, dampening it with water from his canteen before dabbing at the wound with careful precision.

Rebecca sucked in a sharp breath as the cloth touched her skin, the sting of the wound only intensified by the pressure of his hand steadying hers. She fought to keep her face impassive, unwilling to give him the satisfaction of seeing her discomfort.

"Not so tough now, are we?" Nolan's voice was low, a faint hint of amusement creeping back in, though his gaze remained on her hand.

She shot him a withering look. "Just trying to keep from punching the guy who's supposed to be saving my life."

"Oh, trust me, Doc," he replied, smirking as he wrapped the cloth around her hand with practiced ease. "Wouldn't be the first time someone took a swing at me. Though they usually wait until I've finished playing doctor."

A reluctant smile tugged at her lips despite herself. "I'll keep that in mind."

He finished wrapping the makeshift bandage around her hand, his fingers lingering for a moment longer than necessary before he let go. She pulled her hand back, flexing her fingers experimentally. The cloth was snug, steadying the ache in a way that made her breathe a little easier.

"Thanks," she murmured, glancing away as she spoke.

"Don't mention it," he replied, moving back to his place by the window. His voice was casual, but she caught the faintest flicker of something in his eyes before he looked away—a glimmer of something unspoken, something she couldn't quite place.

They lapsed into silence again, each lost in their own thoughts. Rebecca kept her gaze on the dimly lit room, the flickering shadows on the wall, anything to avoid looking at him. She could still feel the warmth of his touch lingering on her skin, an unfamiliar sensation that left her feeling strangely off-balance.

"So, what's a scientist like you doing in a place like this?" His voice broke the silence, his tone laced with irony, but there was a hint of genuine curiosity there too.

She shrugged, forcing herself to keep her expression neutral. "Last time I checked, the world's falling apart. I'd say I'm right where I need to be."

"Guess you're one of those 'save the world' types," he said, an amused edge to his voice. "The kind who thinks one person can make a difference."

She raised an eyebrow, meeting his gaze with a defiant glint in her eye. "And I suppose you're the type who thinks it's all hopeless? That we might as well sit back and watch the world burn?"

Nolan chuckled, shaking his head. "Not exactly. I just don't go around thinking I'm some kind of hero." He leaned back against the wall, his gaze distant. "I've seen enough people trying to 'make a difference' end up in a body bag to know better."

She frowned, a faint prickle of irritation at his cynicism. "Maybe some of us aren't content to just survive. Maybe we want more than that."

For a moment, he was silent, his gaze flickering over her with an unreadable intensity. She felt a strange, fluttering sensation in her chest, a mix of frustration and something she couldn't quite name. He watched her, his expression almost contemplative, as though he were sizing her up, measuring her resolve.

"You're serious," he said finally, his tone almost admiring, though he hid it quickly behind a smirk. "Guess I underestimated you, Doc."

She narrowed her eyes, but there was no malice in his words, just a strange, reluctant respect. "It wouldn't be the first time."

Nolan let out a quiet laugh, the sound warm and unexpectedly genuine. "Touché."

The silence that followed was different, charged with an unspoken understanding, a tentative truce forged in the dim light of the abandoned room. Rebecca could feel her guard slipping, just a little, a faint crack in the walls she'd built around herself. She still didn't trust him—she barely knew him—but there was something about his presence that felt oddly... steadying.

She closed her eyes, exhaling slowly, trying to push away the confusing mix of emotions swirling in her chest. She was here for one reason and one reason only: to survive long enough to deliver the vaccine. She couldn't afford to let her focus slip, not for anyone, least of all this irritating, infuriating man with his sarcastic charm and his irritating tendency to be there whenever she stumbled.

Nolan shifted, breaking her train of thought. She opened her eyes to find him watching her, his gaze thoughtful, as though he were trying to figure her out. She felt a blush rise to her cheeks and quickly looked away, the weight of his gaze unsettling in a way she hadn't anticipated.

"Well," she said, clearing her throat, "I suppose we should get some rest if we're going to keep up this pace tomorrow."

Nolan nodded, his expression neutral once more. "You get some sleep. I'll keep watch."

She hesitated, glancing at him with a mix of suspicion and gratitude. "You sure?"

He shrugged, a faint smile tugging at the corner of his mouth. "What can I say? I'm just a natural-born protector."

She rolled her eyes, but the hint of a smile played at her lips as she settled down, pulling her bag close. As she closed her eyes, the last thing she saw was Nolan's silhouette by the window, his figure steady and unyielding against the shadows. And for the first time in a long time, she felt a flicker of safety, a faint, fragile sense of trust she couldn't quite explain.

Chapter 5: "The First Loss"

The air was heavy with the smell of sweat and dust, mingling with the faint stench of decay that clung to the broken remnants of the city. They had made camp in a derelict warehouse on the outskirts, its walls riddled with holes and rusted beams jutting out like the ribs of some long-dead beast. Inside, Nolan, Rebecca, and their recently acquired group of survivors gathered around a makeshift table of crates, each face etched with exhaustion and wariness.

Across from Rebecca sat Grant, a wiry man in his forties, whose sunken eyes and scarred hands spoke to years of surviving in this unforgiving wasteland. He'd been a mechanic, he claimed, back when cars still ran, and he seemed to think this was his ticket to leading any group he joined.

"This place is as good as we're gonna get," Grant said, glancing at each person with a gaze that brooked no argument. "It's secure enough, and we've got a clear line of sight on anyone coming in."

Nolan gave him a hard look. "Secure? You've got a warped sense of security, friend. We might as well hang a welcome sign out front for Lucifer's hunters."

Grant's lips twisted into a sneer, his gaze narrowing as he met Nolan's steady glare. "If you've got a better idea, soldier boy, I'd love to hear it."

The tension between the two men was a palpable thing, stretching taut across the table. Rebecca, sitting silently between them, glanced from one to the other, feeling a familiar irritation rise within her. She hadn't signed up to play referee between two oversized egos in the middle of an apocalypse.

"Gentlemen," she cut in, her tone dry, "as thrilling as this power struggle is, maybe we could save it until after we've survived the night?"

Nolan's gaze flicked to her, a hint of amusement breaking through his stern expression. "Fine by me, Doc. Just make sure you stick close—last thing I need is you wandering off and getting yourself killed."

Rebecca rolled her eyes, though she couldn't deny the faint, inexplicable comfort she felt at his words. She leaned back, crossing her arms, as the rest of the group continued discussing their limited options.

In addition to Grant, there was Sarah, a young woman who had managed to survive on her own for months, using little more than a baseball bat and nerves of steel. Next to her sat Miguel, a quiet man with a haunted look in his eyes, who rarely spoke but carried a battered pistol that looked like it had been through hell and back.

They were a ragtag group, each person hardened by the unforgiving reality of survival. And yet, despite the weariness and distrust that hung between them, there was an unspoken understanding, a thread that bound them together in their shared struggle.

As the night wore on, the conversation drifted, settling into a tense silence. Outside, the wind howled, rattling the broken windows and filling the air with a hollow, mournful sound. Rebecca closed her eyes, trying to rest, though her mind refused to quiet, thoughts spinning with the weight of everything that had happened.

She wasn't sure how long she'd been sitting there when a faint noise pricked at her senses—a distant, rhythmic thud, barely audible over the wind.

Nolan was already on his feet, his posture tense as he scanned the darkened corners of the warehouse. "We've got company," he muttered, his voice low, barely above a whisper.

The others jolted awake, their expressions shifting from exhaustion to sharp, immediate alertness. Grant grabbed his makeshift weapon—a rusted metal pipe—while Sarah gripped her baseball bat, her knuckles white.

Rebecca's pulse quickened as she reached for the small, worn knife she'd kept in her bag, the weight of it both comforting and terrifying.

"They're coming from the east side," Nolan whispered, nodding toward a narrow corridor that led deeper into the warehouse. "Everyone stay close. We'll move together."

But as they started down the corridor, the first shot rang out, shattering the tense silence. One of Lucifer's hunters had slipped into the building, his rifle raised, his face twisted into a predatory smile. The air exploded with the sounds of gunfire, and Rebecca ducked, her heart pounding as the group scattered for cover.

Miguel returned fire, his pistol spitting bullets at the shadows moving in the dark. Grant swung his metal pipe with a fierce growl, striking one of the hunters as he charged forward. The hunter staggered, blood spilling from his mouth as he fell, but his victory was short-lived. Another hunter moved in, swift and silent, his knife flashing as he slashed across Grant's chest.

Rebecca's breath caught as she watched Grant stagger, blood blooming across his shirt. He dropped to his knees, his eyes wide with shock before they dimmed, his body crumpling to the ground. She felt a cold numbness spread through her as she watched him fall, the reality of death suddenly, violently close.

"Rebecca, move!" Nolan's voice cut through her shock, snapping her back to the present.

She stumbled forward, barely registering the chaos around her as she followed Nolan, ducking behind a stack of crates. Her chest heaved, and she fought to keep her mind focused, pushing away the gnawing fear that threatened to consume her.

Nolan crouched beside her, his gaze hard and unyielding as he scanned the room. "Stay here," he said, his voice tight with controlled fury. "And for the love of all that's left, *don't move.*"

She nodded, too shaken to argue, as he disappeared into the darkness, his figure blending seamlessly into the shadows. The sound of gunfire and clashing weapons filled the air, each shot a brutal reminder of the reality they faced.

Rebecca clutched her knife, her knuckles white, her gaze fixed on the dimly lit room as the battle raged around her. She felt a strange detachment, as though she were watching from a distance, her mind struggling to process the violence unfolding before her.

Then, in a sudden, brutal moment, she saw Sarah go down, her scream cut short as one of the hunters struck her with the butt of his rifle. Rebecca's stomach twisted as she watched the young woman fall, her body crumpling to the ground, lifeless.

A cold fury ignited within her, a raw, pulsing anger that drove away the fear. These people—these hunters—they were little more than animals, taking lives with a callous disregard that left her sickened.

Nolan reappeared beside her, his face grim, his gaze flickering to where Sarah's body lay. For a brief moment, she saw something flicker in his eyes—a crack in his steely exterior, a glimpse of something darker, deeper.

He swore under his breath, the words barely audible, but the anger in his voice was unmistakable.

"They just keep coming," he muttered, his tone cold, deadly. His hand tightened on his rifle, his knuckles white as he glared at the remaining hunters with a look that could have scorched the earth.

Rebecca felt an inexplicable surge of sympathy as she watched him, her own anger mirrored in his expression. She could see the strain in his posture, the way his jaw clenched as though he were holding back a tidal wave of emotions. For the first time, she found herself seeing him as more than just a soldier, more than the sarcastic, unyielding protector she'd come to know.

In that moment, he looked... haunted.

The thought unsettled her, a strange twist in her chest that she didn't have time to examine.

"We need to move," he said abruptly, his voice laced with urgency. "There's too many of them, and we're down to half our group."

Rebecca glanced around, noting that Miguel was still standing, though he looked worse for wear, his face pale and strained. She took a steadying breath, nodding as she met Nolan's gaze.

Together, they moved through the shadows, making their way toward a side exit. The sounds of battle faded behind them, though the tension lingered, a heavy weight pressing down on her chest.

They burst out into the night air, the cool breeze a stark contrast to the stifling heat of the warehouse. Rebecca gasped, her lungs filling with the fresh air as they staggered away from the building, her mind reeling from the events that had just unfolded.

Nolan was beside her, his face impassive, though she could see the tightness in his jaw, the lingering fury that simmered beneath his calm exterior.

"Are you okay?" she asked, her voice barely more than a whisper.

He didn't look at her, his gaze fixed on the distant lights of the city. "Fine."

But she could hear the strain in his voice, the brittle edge that betrayed his attempt at composure. She hesitated, unsure of what to say, but the words slipped out before she could stop them.

"I'm... sorry. About Grant. And Sarah."

His gaze flicked to her, surprise flashing in his eyes before it was quickly masked. He nodded, his expression unreadable as he looked away again. "They knew the risks."

The words were cold, almost detached, but Rebecca sensed the underlying grief, the anger that simmered just beneath the surface. She watched him for a moment, her own heart heavy with the weight of their losses.

For a fleeting moment, she allowed herself to wonder what kind of past had forged this man, what kind of pain he carried with him beneath that unbreakable exterior. She knew better than to ask, but the thought lingered, a faint echo of curiosity that she couldn't quite ignore.

They fell into silence, each lost in their own thoughts as they made their way through the darkened streets. The losses they had suffered hung between them, an unspoken bond that drew them closer, even as they remained distant, each unwilling to bridge the gap that separated them.

And as they walked, Rebecca couldn't help but steal a glance at him, wondering just how deeply those losses had cut—and knowing that, for now, those were wounds he wouldn't let anyone see.

Chapter 6: "Escape Across the Desert"

The Mojave Desert sprawled out before them, an endless stretch of scorched earth and jagged rocks baking under the unforgiving sun. Heat waves shimmered off the sand, and every breath Rebecca took seemed to fill her lungs with fire. The air was heavy, thick with the scent of dust and desolation, and each step felt like dragging herself through a furnace. She could practically feel the desert sapping her strength, greedily pulling her energy into its parched, cracked ground.

Ahead of her, Nolan moved with a steady, relentless pace, his gaze fixed on the horizon as if sheer willpower alone would carry them forward. His rifle was slung across his back, his figure tense and unyielding, every movement precise and efficient, even after hours of walking under the relentless sun.

Rebecca pushed herself to keep up, her breaths coming in ragged gasps as she struggled to ignore the ache in her limbs. She tried to distract herself, glancing around at the barren landscape, the skeletal remains of what might have once been trees, the occasional rusted-out shell of a car half-buried in the sand—a grim reminder of those who had tried and failed to survive this wasteland.

"You're slowing down," Nolan's voice cut through the silence, flat and unapologetic.

She shot him a glare, though it felt like more effort than it was worth. "Not everyone can keep up this endless soldier march, you know," she replied, her voice tinged with irritation. "Some of us are mere mortals."

Nolan's mouth twitched, a hint of amusement flickering across his face. "Didn't realize scientists came with such delicate constitutions," he remarked, casting a sidelong glance at her. "You want me to carry you, Doctor?"

Rebecca scowled, though the idea of rest—of even just stopping for a moment—was so tempting she had to fight to keep her expression defiant. "I'll survive," she muttered, more to herself than to him.

They continued in silence, each step dragging with the weight of exhaustion, the sand slipping beneath her boots, making her footing unsteady. She clenched her jaw, forcing herself to keep going, but every movement felt like a monumental effort, her muscles aching, her skin sticky with sweat.

After what felt like an eternity, Nolan finally called a halt, gesturing toward a small, rocky outcrop that offered a sliver of shade. Rebecca practically collapsed against the rock, leaning her head back and closing her eyes, savoring even the faintest hint of relief from the sun.

When she opened her eyes, she found Nolan watching her, his gaze assessing, as though measuring her strength. She bristled under his scrutiny, meeting his gaze with a defiant look.

"You know," she said, her tone dripping with sarcasm, "you could try looking less...smug about the whole 'not dying of heat exhaustion' thing."

Nolan raised an eyebrow, his expression a mixture of amusement and exasperation. "Smug? Doc, I'm not smug. I'm just...prepared."

"Oh, of course," she replied, her voice thick with irony. "The noble soldier, stoic and unbreakable. Heaven forbid you ever sweat like the rest of us."

He smirked, crossing his arms as he leaned back against the rock. "Believe it or not, I'm just as miserable as you. I just don't see the point in complaining about it every five minutes."

"Who's complaining?" Rebecca shot back, folding her arms tightly. "I'm merely stating the obvious—that you have a talent for making this situation even more unbearable."

He chuckled softly, shaking his head. "Well, I'm sorry for not making your post-apocalyptic desert trek more enjoyable, Doc. Maybe next time, I'll arrange a scenic route."

Rebecca rolled her eyes, though she couldn't help the faint, grudging smile tugging at her lips. Despite the exhaustion, despite the heat, there was something oddly... reassuring about his sarcasm. It was familiar, grounding, even as it drove her to frustration.

They rested in silence for a few minutes, each lost in their thoughts. But the stillness of the desert had a strange way of amplifying everything—the distant hum of insects, the whisper of the wind against the rocks, the steady rhythm of her own breathing. She felt acutely aware of every detail, every sound, every subtle shift in the air.

When they resumed their march, the silence between them was heavier, more charged. Rebecca kept her gaze focused on the ground, the endless stretch of sand and rock blurring together as her mind drifted, lulled by the monotony of their steps.

That's when she heard it—a low, guttural snarl that sent a cold shiver down her spine.

She looked up, her heart skipping a beat as she caught sight of a figure in the distance, stumbling toward them with an unnatural, jerking gait. Its skin was gray and mottled, its eyes empty and glassy, fixed on them with a mindless hunger. Rebecca's breath caught as she realized what she was seeing.

Infected.

Before she could react, another snarl echoed from her right, followed by the unmistakable shuffling of more infected, their bodies lurching out from behind a cluster of rocks. Her stomach twisted as she counted at least four, maybe five, each one closing in on them with an eerie, relentless determination.

"Nolan—" she began, her voice catching as she took a step back, her mind racing.

He was already in motion, his rifle in hand, his expression cold and focused. "Get behind me," he ordered, his tone leaving no room for argument.

Rebecca hesitated, a surge of pride and frustration flaring within her, but survival instincts overrode everything else. She moved behind him, her pulse pounding in her ears as she watched him raise his rifle, his movements swift and practiced.

The first shot rang out, shattering the stillness of the desert. One of the infected dropped, its skull exploding in a sickening spray of blackened blood. The others barely seemed to register the loss, their eyes still fixed on Rebecca, their bodies jerking forward with an almost mechanical precision.

Nolan fired again, and another infected went down, its body crumpling in the sand. But more were closing in, their snarls filling the air, their hands reaching out with claw-like fingers.

Rebecca felt a surge of panic as one of them broke away from the pack, its gaze locking onto her with a single-minded intensity. She took a step back, her hand fumbling for the knife at her belt, her movements clumsy and desperate.

But before she could even draw her weapon, Nolan was there, his arm reaching out to pull her back, his body moving between her and the infected with a speed that took her breath away. She watched, heart in her throat, as he swung his rifle like a club, the butt of it smashing into the creature's head with a sickening crunch.

The infected collapsed, twitching in the sand, and Nolan turned, his gaze fierce as he took in the remaining attackers. His face was set in a grim expression, his jaw clenched, his movements precise and deadly. For a brief moment, Rebecca saw him not as the sarcastic, infuriating man she'd come to know, but as a soldier—a warrior, hardened and unyielding, a man who had survived too many battles and lost too much to back down now.

When the last infected fell, silence settled over them, broken only by the faint whisper of the wind. Nolan lowered his rifle, his shoulders tense, his breathing steady but labored. He glanced back at her, his gaze sharp and assessing, as though checking to see if she was unharmed.

"You okay?" he asked, his voice rough, almost gentle.

Rebecca swallowed, nodding as she tried to steady her racing heart. "I'm...fine."

He nodded, his gaze lingering on her for a moment before he turned away, his expression unreadable. She watched him, a strange, unsettling mix of emotions swirling within her—gratitude, frustration, and something else, something deeper that she couldn't quite name.

They resumed their march, each step dragging with the weight of exhaustion and the lingering tension of the attack. The sun was setting now, casting long shadows across the desert, the air cooling as darkness crept over the landscape.

By the time they found a small, sheltered alcove to camp for the night, Rebecca could barely keep her eyes open. She sank down against the cool rock, her body aching, her mind fogged with fatigue.

Nolan sat a few feet away, his gaze fixed on the horizon as he kept watch, his figure outlined by the faint glow of the moon. She watched him through half-lidded eyes, her thoughts drifting, her mind heavy with exhaustion.

As she drifted off to sleep, her dreams were filled with fragments—memories blurred by the haze of sleep, images that shifted and changed with a strange, dreamlike logic. She saw herself stumbling in the desert, the sun blazing overhead, her limbs heavy with exhaustion.

And then she saw Nolan, his face half-shadowed, his expression fierce as he reached out to pull her back from the edge. His hand was warm, steady, his gaze filled with a quiet intensity that sent a strange, fluttering warmth through her chest. In the dream, he looked at her with an expression she couldn't quite understand—an expression that was both protective and... caring.

Rebecca stirred, her brow furrowing as the dream shifted, the images slipping away like sand through her fingers. But the feeling lingered, a faint, inexplicable warmth that left her feeling strangely unsettled.

When she awoke, the first light of dawn was creeping over the horizon, casting a pale, silvery glow across the desert. Nolan was still there, his figure silhouetted against the morning light, his gaze fixed on the distance, as if he were searching for something just out of reach.

Rebecca watched him for a moment, the memory of her dream still fresh in her mind. She felt a strange pang of emotion, a flicker of something she couldn't quite place. She pushed the thought aside, forcing herself to focus on the reality before her.

This was Nolan—stoic, sarcastic, infuriating Nolan. And she was just as wary of him as ever.

But as she got to her feet, brushing the sand from her clothes, she couldn't shake the feeling that something had shifted between them. It was subtle, almost imperceptible, but it was there—a faint crack in the wall she'd built around herself, a tiny opening that left her feeling exposed, vulnerable.

She forced a smile, hoping to mask the strange, lingering warmth that still pulsed in her chest. "Ready for another day of endless walking?" she asked, her voice light, almost mocking.

Nolan glanced at her, his expression as unreadable as ever. "Only if you promise not to faint halfway through."

Rebecca rolled her eyes, her irritation flaring back to life, grounding her in the familiar, the safe. "I'll do my best not to inconvenience you, Captain."

He smirked, his gaze lingering on her for a moment before he turned away. "Appreciate it."

They fell into step beside each other, the silence settling over them like a fragile truce. And as they walked, Rebecca found herself glancing at him, wondering, just for a moment, what it was that lay hidden beneath his guarded exterior—and why, despite everything, she felt a faint, inexplicable pull toward him.

Chapter 7: "On the Edge of Survival"

The small, broken-down cabin they stumbled upon felt like nothing short of a miracle. Its faded wooden walls leaned at odd angles, and the roof looked as though a stiff breeze might blow it away, but to Rebecca and Nolan, it was sanctuary. With night rapidly approaching, the only other option was to keep going and risk collapsing under the stars—a far less appealing choice.

Rebecca leaned against the doorframe, catching her breath. Every part of her body ached, and her stomach gave an involuntary growl as if to remind her of the scarcity of food they'd managed to scrounge up. The cabin, unfortunately, hadn't come with a hidden stockpile of supplies. A quick search had revealed little more than a dusty tin cup and some brittle wooden planks that might serve as a barricade.

"Well," she muttered, eyeing the flimsy door that barely latched shut, "this is...cozy."

Nolan gave a snort, tossing his bag onto the floor with a tired sigh. "Cozy, sure," he replied, his voice heavy with sarcasm. "It's got all the charm of a tomb."

Rebecca managed a dry laugh. "Maybe because we're about two rations away from joining the dead ourselves?"

Nolan smirked, but she could see the exhaustion shadowing his eyes, deeper and darker than she'd ever seen it. She wanted to say something—maybe a word of encouragement, though what that would look like, she had no idea—but he turned away, rummaging through his bag in search of any food they hadn't yet exhausted.

"Here." He handed her a half-crushed protein bar, looking only mildly apologetic. "Our last meal, if we're lucky."

Rebecca took it, breaking it in half. The bar was dry and tasteless, more cardboard than anything, but at this point, even a single crumb felt like a feast. She took a bite, chewing slowly, trying not to think too much about what they'd do come morning.

They ate in silence, the quiet interrupted only by the distant sounds of the desert night: the occasional wail of the wind, the whisper of sand shifting outside. Rebecca closed her eyes, her mind drifting, her body craving sleep even as her nerves kept her alert. The floor was hard beneath her, the thin blanket she'd found offering little comfort.

Out of the corner of her eye, she noticed Nolan shift, his posture tense as he adjusted his arm. She frowned, studying him. In the dim light, she could see the subtle clench of his jaw, the way he pressed a hand to his shoulder. He winced, ever so slightly, as if trying to hide the movement.

She watched him for a moment, feeling a faint, unexpected tug of concern.

"Nolan," she said quietly, her voice breaking the stillness. "Are you...okay?"

He looked at her, his expression carefully neutral. "Fine," he said, though the strain in his voice betrayed him.

She gave him a pointed look, tilting her head. "You don't look fine. And considering the hell we've just walked through, I'm guessing you've got more than a couple of new bruises."

He shrugged, though the movement was stiff, pained. "Just an old injury. It's nothing."

"Nothing?" She raised an eyebrow, not buying it for a second. "You've been holding that arm like it's about to fall off. Let me take a look."

Nolan's eyes flickered with something unreadable, and for a moment, she thought he might argue. But then, perhaps from sheer exhaustion, he relented, letting out a sigh as he shifted to sit with his back against the wall. He rolled up his sleeve, revealing a scarred patch of skin on his shoulder that looked angry and red, an old wound that had been aggravated by days of trekking through unforgiving terrain.

Rebecca bit her lip, suppressing the rush of sympathy that threatened to bubble up. She reached into her bag, rummaging for the last of their medical supplies—just a small, nearly empty bottle of antiseptic and a few strips of cloth she could use as a makeshift bandage.

"This might sting," she warned, unscrewing the cap.

He gave a short, humorless laugh. "After the last few days, I think I can handle it."

Rebecca didn't respond, focusing instead on her task. She soaked a bit of cloth with the antiseptic, dabbing it carefully over the wound. He tensed under her touch, his muscles tight with restraint, though he made no sound.

The silence between them grew thick, tense, the only sound the faint rustle of fabric as she worked. Rebecca found herself hyper-aware of his presence, the heat radiating from him, the steady rise and fall of his breathing. She swallowed, feeling an unfamiliar warmth creep into her cheeks.

Nolan looked down at her, his gaze intense, watching her with an unreadable expression as she wrapped the cloth around his shoulder. She forced herself to focus, her fingers brushing his skin as she tied the makeshift bandage.

"There," she said softly, tying the last knot. "That should hold until we find something better."

For a moment, neither of them moved, their gazes locked. She was all too aware of his closeness, the subtle tension in his posture, the faint, lingering warmth of his hand resting on his knee beside her. It was as though the air itself had shifted, thickened, wrapping around them in an unspoken, fragile connection that felt both exhilarating and terrifying.

"Thanks," he murmured, his voice barely above a whisper.

Rebecca gave a quick, almost nervous nod, breaking the spell as she drew back, retreating to her side of the room. She felt her heart pounding, an inexplicable, traitorous flutter that left her feeling breathless and unsettled.

They sat in silence, each lost in their own thoughts, the tension between them an almost physical presence in the small, cramped space. Rebecca closed her eyes, trying to push away the memory of his touch, the way his skin had felt warm beneath her fingers, steady, solid.

After a while, she glanced over, catching a glimpse of him with his head resting against the wall, his gaze distant, his face softened by a weariness that cut through his usual stoicism. She felt an unexpected pang, a faint ache in her chest that she couldn't quite explain.

Shaking her head, she turned away, pulling her blanket up and settling into a restless, uneasy sleep.

In her sleep, Rebecca found herself once again in the desert, her steps heavy, the sun beating down on her with a brutal intensity. She felt the weight of exhaustion, the ache in her bones, the endless, unyielding stretch of sand pressing down on her, suffocating her.

But then, through the haze, she saw him—Nolan, standing beside her, his hand reaching out, steadying her, his expression softened by a strange, unexpected tenderness. He looked at her with a quiet, fierce concern, his gaze piercing, grounding.

She felt a warmth spread through her, an unfamiliar, dizzying sensation that made her heart race. His hand was warm against her arm, solid, anchoring her in a way that felt both terrifying and comforting. He looked at her, his eyes filled with something she couldn't quite name, something that left her feeling exposed, vulnerable.

The desert around them faded, replaced by the dim glow of the cabin, the rough wooden walls, the soft rustle of fabric as he moved beside her. She could feel his presence, close, warm, his hand lingering on her shoulder, his gaze intense, filled with a silent understanding that left her breathless.

She wanted to reach out, to bridge the distance, to say something—anything—but the words slipped away, lost in the quiet, the stillness, the weight of his gaze.

Rebecca woke with a start, her heart pounding, her mind fogged with sleep. She blinked, disoriented, the memory of the dream still fresh in her mind, lingering like the echo of a heartbeat. She glanced over at Nolan, who was still resting against the wall, his gaze distant, his expression unreadable.

She felt a flush rise to her cheeks, a strange, inexplicable warmth that left her feeling exposed, vulnerable. She forced herself to look away, pushing down the lingering remnants of the dream, the unsettling sense of… something she couldn't quite place.

"Morning," he murmured, his voice low, rough with sleep.

She managed a nod, hoping her voice sounded steady. "Morning."

They packed in silence, the tension between them heavier, charged with an unspoken understanding that neither of them dared acknowledge. As they stepped out into the cool morning air, the desert stretching out before them, Rebecca couldn't shake the feeling that something had shifted between them—a subtle, fragile connection, a crack in the wall she'd built around herself.

And as they set off once again, the dream lingered in her mind, a faint, unsettling reminder of the strange, undeniable pull that seemed to bind them together, fragile and unspoken, but there all the same.

Chapter 8: "Moments of Peace"

They had been trekking up the mountains for most of the morning, the rocky trail winding beneath a sky that finally seemed kinder, cooler. Sunlight filtered through the leaves, casting shifting patterns across the ground. It was a blessed change from the relentless desert heat, and despite the strain of the climb, the mountain air felt like a balm to Rebecca's lungs.

Ahead of her, Nolan moved with an ease that suggested he was made for this kind of terrain. She found herself watching him as he picked his way up the rocky path, his steps sure and unhurried, his body blending into the rugged landscape as though he belonged there.

When they finally reached a clearing near the top, Nolan paused, scanning the area with a practiced eye. Satisfied, he nodded toward a small alcove tucked beneath an overhang of rock, sheltered by a dense cluster of trees.

"Perfect spot," he said, setting down his pack and taking a deep breath. "We'll stop here for a bit."

Rebecca gave a grateful sigh, dropping down onto a flat patch of grass and letting herself relax for the first time in days. The mountain air was fresh and cool, a breeze stirring through the trees, carrying with it the faint scent of pine. For the first time since this endless journey began, she felt... almost human.

Nolan, true to form, didn't waste time resting. He was already busy gathering small branches and dried leaves, moving with the quiet efficiency she had come to recognize. She watched him for a moment, feeling a mix of gratitude and curiosity.

"You know, you're making the rest of us look bad with all this boundless energy," she called out, leaning back on her elbows as she watched him.

He looked up, smirking. "It's called survival skills, Doc. Maybe you've heard of them?"

Rebecca raised an eyebrow, giving him an unimpressed look. "Survival skills, sure. I just didn't realize you could turn them into an Olympic sport."

"Oh, there's a lot you don't know about survival," he shot back, his tone laced with a familiar, teasing sarcasm. "Stick around, and you might just learn a thing or two."

"Is that an offer to teach me?" she asked, surprised by her own daring.

He paused, considering her with an expression that was half-amusement, half-serious. "Depends. You think you're up for it?"

"Try me."

Nolan chuckled, the sound warm and unexpectedly genuine. "Alright, Doc. First rule of survival in the wilderness: know how to start a fire. Here." He tossed a small pile of dried twigs and leaves her way, nodding toward them as he crouched down beside her. "Think you can handle that?"

Rebecca stared down at the makeshift pile of kindling, raising an eyebrow. "I'm not exactly 'Survivor' material, but I'll give it a shot."

He handed her a flint, his fingers brushing hers in a way that felt casual, yet somehow lingered a beat longer than it should have. She swallowed, focusing on the task at hand as she fumbled with the flint, trying to remember what little she knew about starting a fire.

Nolan watched her, amusement dancing in his eyes. "Strike it like this," he demonstrated, his hand covering hers, guiding her fingers with a steady pressure. She could feel the warmth of his hand, the calluses on his fingertips, rough yet somehow reassuring. She followed his lead, striking the flint against the stone, watching as sparks flew, catching the dry leaves with a faint, flickering glow.

"There you go," he murmured, his voice low, as though he didn't want to disturb the fragile flame that slowly came to life. "Not bad for a scientist."

She shot him a look, smirking. "I guess there's hope for me yet."

They watched the fire grow, small but steady, crackling softly in the quiet of the clearing. Nolan leaned back, his gaze fixed on the flames, his face softened by the warm light. Rebecca felt a strange calm settle over her, a feeling of safety that was so rare, so fleeting in this harsh world, it almost felt surreal.

She looked around, taking in the mountains, the soft whisper of the trees, the way the sunlight filtered through the leaves, casting dappled shadows across the ground. For the first time in what felt like forever, there was no danger lurking around the corner, no sense of impending doom pressing down on her.

"This place…" she murmured, almost to herself. "It's beautiful. Hard to believe there's anything wrong with the world when you're up here."

Nolan nodded, his gaze distant, thoughtful. "It's easy to forget, sometimes. That there's still something good left." His voice was quiet, almost reverent, as though he were speaking to himself rather than to her.

They sat in companionable silence, each lost in their own thoughts, the fire crackling softly between them. Rebecca felt a warmth settle over her, not just from the flames, but from the simple, human presence beside her. She glanced over at Nolan, her gaze lingering on him, a quiet curiosity stirring within her.

He caught her looking, raising an eyebrow. "What?"

She shook her head, smiling. "Nothing. Just trying to picture you in a lab coat."

Nolan snorted, the sound unexpectedly boyish. "Now that's an image no one needs. Me in a lab coat? Can't say science is really my thing, Doc."

"Shocking revelation," she replied, her tone dry. "I don't know—maybe you've got a hidden scientist in there somewhere."

"Doubtful." He chuckled, shaking his head. "I'll leave the lab stuff to you. I'm more of the 'make fire, avoid getting killed' type."

"Useful skills," she admitted, laughing. "Guess we're not so different after all."

Nolan tilted his head, studying her with an expression she couldn't quite read. "Not so different, huh? That's a new one."

She shrugged, a smile tugging at her lips. "Survival brings out some strange similarities, I guess."

He nodded, his gaze lingering on her for a moment longer than necessary, his eyes softening in a way that sent an unexpected warmth flooding through her. There was a quiet intensity in his gaze, a depth she hadn't noticed before, as though he were seeing her in a different light.

And in that moment, something shifted.

Neither of them moved, the air between them charged with a subtle, unspoken tension that crackled like the fire at their feet. Rebecca felt her pulse quicken, a warmth rising in her chest that she couldn't quite explain. She held his gaze, her breath catching as the silence stretched, deepened, drawing them closer in a way that felt both exhilarating and terrifying.

Almost without thinking, she leaned in, the movement so slight, so tentative, she wasn't sure she'd even meant to do it. But Nolan didn't pull away. His gaze softened, his lips curving into a faint, surprised smile as he leaned in, closing the distance between them.

The kiss was gentle, tentative—a whisper of warmth, a brief, fragile connection that felt both thrilling and achingly tender. His hand brushed her cheek, his touch light, almost reverent, as though he were afraid to break the spell that had settled over them.

They pulled back, both of them startled, as if waking from a dream. Rebecca felt her cheeks flush, a faint, traitorous warmth spreading through her, leaving her feeling breathless, vulnerable.

Nolan looked away, clearing his throat, a faint smile tugging at the corner of his mouth. "Well," he said, his voice rough, teasing. "Didn't see that coming, did you?"

She laughed, the sound a little shaky, though she couldn't help the smile that spread across her face. "No," she admitted, a touch of irony in her voice. "Not exactly what I expected from a survival lesson."

"Guess I'm full of surprises," he murmured, his gaze flicking back to hers, a glint of warmth and something unspoken lingering in his eyes.

They settled back into silence, the air between them charged, different now, as though something unspoken had passed between them, shifting the ground beneath their feet. Rebecca felt a strange, quiet thrill in her chest, a warmth that lingered, that left her feeling both comforted and unsteady.

But they didn't speak of it. Whatever it was, whatever had just happened between them, it remained unacknowledged, a silent understanding shared in the quiet of the mountains, as fleeting and fragile as the flickering flames.

Chapter 9: "Betrayal in the Shadows"

The afternoon sun cast long shadows over the mountainside, bathing the landscape in a dusty, golden light that made everything seem deceptively calm. Rebecca's attention was fixed on the delicate vial she held in her hands, the vaccine sample catching the light as she turned it over, studying its faint blue glow. They'd reached another temporary campsite, this one tucked into a sheltered canyon, providing a brief respite from the harsh journey.

She barely registered the sounds of Nolan and the others moving around camp, lost in the comforting familiarity of her work. The task grounded her, a reminder of the mission, of why they were enduring this endless, perilous journey. But a prickling sense of unease lingered, a tension in the air that seemed to have settled over the group since dawn. She couldn't quite shake the feeling that something was... wrong.

A sudden, sharp pain bloomed in her side, cutting off her thoughts. Her breath hitched, her body tensing as she felt something cold and hard press against her ribs. She looked down, shock flooding her system as she saw a blade's edge glinting under her jacket. Her gaze snapped up, locking onto the dark, unyielding eyes of Miguel, one of the quietest members of their group, who now wore an expression she'd never seen before—one of icy, detached purpose.

"Miguel?" she whispered, her mind struggling to process what was happening, her voice tight with disbelief.

He gave her a cold smile, one that sent a chill through her. "Sorry, Doctor. Orders are orders."

Rebecca barely had time to react before he yanked the vial from her grip, pocketing it with swift precision. She staggered back, her hand going to her side as the blade sliced through her jacket, leaving a fiery line of pain across her ribs. Panic surged, her mind racing, but she forced herself to remain calm, her gaze fixed on Miguel as he slipped back into the shadows.

"Miguel, wait—" she began, her voice low, pleading, but he was already gone, his footsteps disappearing into the trees.

Before she could process what had happened, Nolan appeared, his gaze zeroing in on her with a sharpness that cut through her haze of shock. His eyes darkened as he took in the blood seeping through her jacket, the torn fabric where the knife had cut her.

"Rebecca," he said, his voice a low growl, his tone edged with a fury that she felt more than heard. "What the hell happened?"

She pressed a hand to her side, wincing as the pain flared again. "Miguel," she managed, her voice tight. "He—he took one of the vials."

Nolan's expression shifted from anger to something darker, more dangerous. Without another word, he grabbed his rifle and took off in the direction Miguel had gone, his movements sharp, purposeful, every step laced with a barely restrained fury.

Rebecca tried to follow, but the pain in her side flared, forcing her to stop, her vision blurring as she pressed her hand harder against the wound. She could hear Nolan's footsteps fading into the distance, the silence of the forest swallowing him up.

She sank to her knees, her breaths coming in short, shallow gasps as she fought to keep the pain at bay. She forced herself to stay calm, her mind racing as she tried to process the betrayal, the shock of seeing Miguel—the quiet, unassuming man who had been with them since the beginning—turn on them with such cold calculation.

Minutes passed, maybe more, before she heard footsteps approaching. She tensed, her heart pounding, but relief washed over her as Nolan's figure appeared through the trees. His expression was dark, his jaw clenched, every line of his body radiating barely contained anger.

"He's gone," he muttered, his voice a low, frustrated growl. "Slipped out of sight. Must've known the terrain."

Rebecca nodded, biting back the ache that pulsed in her side. "I didn't... I didn't see it coming," she admitted, her voice a mix of anger and disbelief. "He barely spoke to any of us. How could we have missed it?"

Nolan knelt down beside her, his expression softening as he took in her pallor, the way she clutched at her side. "You're hurt," he said quietly, his gaze flicking to her side. He reached out, pulling her hand away to inspect the wound, his touch surprisingly gentle as he peeled back the fabric to examine the cut.

"It's not deep," she managed, though her voice wavered as the pain flared. "Just... a scratch, really."

"Right," he muttered, his tone sardonic, though she could see the worry flickering in his eyes. "And I suppose 'just a scratch' explains why you're practically turning green."

She rolled her eyes, though the effort nearly sent her vision spinning. "I'm fine, Captain. Just need a moment to... gather myself."

"Uh-huh. Keep telling yourself that." His tone was sharp, but there was a tenderness in his movements as he tore a strip of fabric from his shirt, pressing it carefully against the wound to stop the bleeding. She held her breath, feeling the warmth of his hand through the fabric, the steady pressure that grounded her, kept her anchored.

"Why do you do that?" she murmured, her voice barely a whisper.

He glanced at her, one eyebrow raised. "Do what?"

"Act like you're immune to... to caring about anyone. You don't have to help me, you know."

He held her gaze for a long moment, his expression unreadable. "Just because I don't say it doesn't mean I don't care, Doc," he said, his voice low, almost a murmur. His gaze flicked away, his fingers lingering on her wound a second longer than necessary before he pulled back.

Rebecca's heart gave a strange, traitorous flutter at his words, the subtle warmth in his tone, the unspoken tension that hung between them. She forced herself to look away, biting back the feelings that bubbled up, the confusing, disorienting mix of emotions that left her feeling more vulnerable than the wound itself.

But as Nolan worked, his hands steady and his touch careful, she felt a strange sense of comfort, a feeling she couldn't quite explain. She closed her eyes, letting herself sink into the moment, the warmth of his presence, the strength in his hands, the quiet assurance that he was there, beside her.

When he finished, he leaned back, his expression softening as he looked at her. "There," he said, his tone light, almost teasing. "Good as new. Though you might want to steer clear of any more knife-wielding friends."

She managed a faint smile, her gaze meeting his. "I'll do my best. Maybe you should just keep them all at bay, since you're so good at it."

He chuckled, though there was a hardness in his eyes that betrayed his amusement. "Don't worry, Doc. From now on, no one gets close to you without my permission."

The words hung in the air, charged with an intensity that neither of them acknowledged, yet both felt. Rebecca looked away, feeling her cheeks warm, a subtle tension settling between them, fragile yet undeniable.

As they sat in silence, the weight of the betrayal lingered, a bitter reminder of the dangers that surrounded them. But in that moment, with Nolan's quiet presence beside her, Rebecca felt an unexpected sense of security, a feeling that, despite everything, they would make it through.

And for now, that was enough.

Chapter 10: "Coming Closer"

The mountains stretched around them in quiet majesty, the world falling into an eerie silence as dusk crept over the horizon. They'd managed to find a small shelter, a rock-formed alcove nestled into the mountainside, hidden from view and mercifully shielded from the wind. Rebecca sank onto a rough patch of ground, feeling a strange, welcome relief wash over her as she allowed herself to breathe, just for a moment.

Nolan crouched beside her, his gaze sweeping over the landscape before he finally relaxed, the tension in his shoulders easing as he sat back, stretching his legs out. For once, they were alone, truly alone, with no signs of pursuit, no haunting shadows. It was just the two of them and the soft, steady rhythm of their breathing against the whispering wind.

Rebecca leaned her head back, letting her gaze drift up to the sky, the first stars appearing against the deepening blue. She felt a strange sense of peace, an almost fragile quiet that settled over her like a warm blanket, soothing the constant edge of anxiety that had clung to her since they'd started this journey.

"Almost makes you forget we're on the run," she murmured, her voice soft, almost wistful.

Nolan glanced over at her, a faint smile tugging at the corner of his mouth. "Almost," he echoed, his tone laced with irony. "But I don't know—just doesn't feel right without someone trying to kill us."

Rebecca laughed, the sound surprising her. It felt like ages since she'd last laughed, a real, unguarded laugh that shook loose the weight of everything pressing down on her.

"Well, Captain," she said, giving him a sidelong glance, "if you're feeling deprived, I'm sure we could find some danger out there to keep you entertained."

Nolan chuckled, shaking his head. "Tempting. But for once, I think I'll take the peace and quiet."

They fell into silence, each of them content to simply sit there, letting the stillness settle over them. Rebecca glanced at him, her gaze lingering as she studied his face, softened in the dim light, free from the constant tension and guardedness that usually marked his features. In this rare, quiet moment, he looked almost... serene.

"You know," she murmured, breaking the silence, "you're different up here."

He raised an eyebrow, glancing at her with mild amusement. "Different how?"

She shrugged, a faint smile playing at her lips. "Less... stoic. Almost like a normal person."

He gave her a look, feigning offense. "Careful, Doc. I might start thinking you actually like having me around."

"Don't get ahead of yourself," she replied, rolling her eyes, though her tone was softened by the smile that lingered on her lips. "I just meant that... well, it's nice to see you relaxed for a change. Even if it is a little unsettling."

He chuckled, the sound low and warm, and she felt a strange warmth spread through her chest, a quiet thrill that left her feeling oddly vulnerable.

They sat in comfortable silence, the soft, natural rhythm of the wilderness settling around them. Rebecca felt a shift, an unspoken understanding that seemed to hum in the air between them. Her gaze drifted to Nolan again, watching as he closed his eyes, his face softened by the faint starlight.

She knew she should look away, that she should guard herself, keep that familiar distance she'd maintained from everyone since this nightmare began. But something about the moment, about the quiet, safe isolation of the mountains, made her feel braver, bolder than she'd felt in a long time.

"Nolan," she murmured, her voice barely a whisper, "why do you keep doing this?"

He opened his eyes, his gaze finding hers in the dim light, a flicker of curiosity there. "Doing what?"

"Risking your life for someone like me," she said, her voice tight, edged with a vulnerability she hadn't intended to show. "You could have walked away so many times. You still could."

He held her gaze, his expression softening, something warm and unreadable flickering in his eyes. "You think I'm the kind of guy who walks away?"

She shook her head, a faint smile tugging at her lips. "No... I think you're the kind of guy who stays. Even when it's probably the harder choice."

He didn't respond, his gaze steady, his eyes tracing over her face in a way that made her heart flutter, leaving her feeling exposed, yet safe, all at once. They sat there in the dim light, the silence stretching between them, heavy and charged, as though the world had faded away, leaving only the two of them in this fragile, intimate bubble.

Without thinking, Rebecca reached out, her hand resting lightly on his arm, her fingers brushing against the rough fabric of his jacket. He didn't pull away; if anything, he leaned into her touch, his gaze softening as he looked at her, a faint, almost wistful smile playing at his lips.

"Rebecca," he murmured, his voice low, almost reverent, as though he were speaking her name for the first time.

She felt her pulse quicken, her breath catching as he reached up, his hand cupping her cheek with a gentleness that took her by surprise. His thumb brushed against her skin, a light, feather-soft touch that sent a shiver through her, leaving her breathless.

Their gazes met, a silent understanding passing between them, an unspoken recognition of something they'd both been holding back, denying for too long. The weight of the moment settled over them, fragile and electric, as though they were on the edge of something vast and uncharted.

And then, slowly, carefully, he leaned in, his lips brushing against hers in a kiss that was soft, tender, filled with a quiet, aching need. She closed her eyes, sinking into the warmth of his touch, the steady strength of his presence, letting herself fall into the moment, forgetting the world, the mission, everything but the feel of him, close and real, grounding her in a way she hadn't thought possible.

The kiss deepened, slow and deliberate, each touch a gentle exploration, a hesitant, cautious surrender. She felt his hand move to the small of her back, his touch warm and steady, anchoring her, making her feel safe, cherished. And in that quiet, stolen moment, she allowed herself to forget, to let go, to simply be.

When they finally pulled back, their breaths mingling in the cool night air, they looked at each other, a quiet wonderment in their eyes, as though they were seeing each other anew.

"Well," she murmured, her voice barely more than a whisper, "that... wasn't in the survival manual."

He chuckled, the sound warm, a hint of relief there, as though he, too, were surprised by the depth of the moment. "No... I don't think they covered that one."

They sat in silence, each of them absorbing the quiet, fragile intimacy they'd shared, the unspoken connection that seemed to hum in the air between them. Rebecca felt a warmth bloom in her chest, a sense of peace she hadn't felt in a long time, as though, for the first time, she'd found something—someone—worth holding onto.

Nolan's gaze softened, his hand lingering on hers, a subtle, unspoken promise in the way he held her, as though he, too, felt the weight of what lay between them, the quiet certainty that whatever came next, they would face it together.

But they didn't speak of it, didn't dare put words to the fragile, precious bond they'd discovered in the quiet of the mountains. Instead, they let the silence settle around them, each content to simply be, to share this fleeting, intimate moment, knowing that, for now, it was enough.

Chapter 11: "False Trail"

The mountain path wound ahead, steep and narrow, flanked by jagged rocks and patches of scrubby brush that rustled with the faintest breeze. The sun was beginning to dip below the horizon, casting long shadows across the trail, making every step feel more ominous, every shift in the air more tense.

Rebecca walked beside Nolan, her focus honed on the path ahead, but the dull ache in her side was becoming harder to ignore. She hadn't complained, not yet, but she could feel her strength waning, her pace lagging slightly as they climbed higher.

Nolan, as if sensing her struggle, slowed his steps, matching her pace without comment, though she caught the brief flicker of concern in his gaze whenever he glanced her way. She resisted the urge to roll her eyes—he'd already shown more care for her well-being than she'd thought him capable of, but she couldn't afford to let her guard slip, not when they were so close to catching the traitor who'd nearly killed her.

The information they'd managed to scrape together led them to a ridge high above the valley, a makeshift hideout built into the mountain, hidden by brush and jagged boulders. It wasn't much, but it was enough to keep someone out of sight—and, Rebecca realized, enough to keep someone from being easily found.

Nolan stopped at the base of the ridge, his gaze narrowed as he surveyed the area. He motioned for Rebecca to stay behind him, his voice low and tense. "If Miguel's holed up here, he'll know we're coming. Stay alert."

Rebecca nodded, her jaw clenched against the pain in her side. "I'm alert," she murmured, her voice edged with irony. "It's not like he tried to kill me or anything."

Nolan shot her a look, somewhere between exasperation and amusement. "Just keep that sharp wit ready. If he jumps out, maybe it'll scare him off."

They crept up the slope, moving with careful precision, their senses heightened as they approached the entrance to the hideout. Every crunch of gravel underfoot, every whisper of wind through the trees felt amplified, charged with the potential for ambush.

At the mouth of the hideout, Nolan pressed a finger to his lips, signaling Rebecca to be silent as he peered around the corner. She held her breath, the tension coiling in her stomach as she watched him survey the area, his movements slow and deliberate.

He pulled back, his voice barely a whisper. "It's empty. For now."

They slipped inside, the darkened cave damp and cool, its walls slick with moisture that dripped down in faint rivulets. The floor was cluttered with discarded supplies—an empty water bottle, a torn blanket, a few scattered papers. Rebecca glanced around, her gaze sharp as she scanned for any sign of the stolen vaccine.

"Anything?" she whispered, keeping her voice low.

Nolan shook his head, his expression tense. "Nothing yet. But he wouldn't have left it lying around."

They moved deeper into the cave, the shadows thickening, their footsteps echoing off the stone walls. The silence was unnerving, broken only by the faint drip of water and the sound of their breathing. Rebecca felt her pulse quicken, her senses on high alert, every instinct screaming that something was wrong.

And then, a faint click sounded from somewhere above them, barely audible but unmistakable.

Nolan's eyes widened, his hand shooting out to grab her arm. "Rebecca—"

Before he could finish, the trap sprang. The ground beneath them gave way, a sharp crack echoing through the cave as a section of the floor collapsed, sending them tumbling down a steep, rocky slope. Rebecca felt the impact jolt through her, her wounded side flaring with pain as she landed, her vision blurring as the world spun around her.

She hit the ground hard, her body aching, her mind struggling to focus as she registered the distant sound of footsteps—someone running, escaping. She forced herself to her feet, her hand pressed to her side as she stumbled forward, her vision swimming.

Nolan was beside her in an instant, his hand steadying her as he glanced back at the path they'd fallen from, his expression a mix of fury and frustration. "Damn it," he muttered, his voice tight with barely restrained anger. "He set us up."

Rebecca managed a faint, wry smile despite the pain. "Well, he didn't exactly leave a welcome mat."

Nolan's jaw clenched, his gaze flicking over her with a look that was far too close to worry. "You're hurt."

"It's... fine," she lied, though the weakness in her voice betrayed her. "Just a little... unplanned tumble."

He gave her a look that clearly said he wasn't buying it, but he didn't press the issue, instead helping her to her feet, his arm steady around her waist as he guided her toward the exit.

They made their way out of the cave, each step sending fresh waves of pain through Rebecca's side, though she bit back any sign of discomfort, unwilling to show just how weak she felt. But Nolan's arm remained around her, his grip firm, steady, as though he could sense her faltering strength.

When they finally reached the outside, he led her to a sheltered spot beneath a cluster of trees, easing her down onto a fallen log as he knelt beside her, his gaze dark with barely restrained worry.

"Stay still," he murmured, his voice soft, but with a hard edge of determination. "Let me look."

She started to protest, but the exhaustion was beginning to catch up to her, sapping her strength, leaving her with little fight left. She nodded, her breath shallow as he carefully pulled back her jacket, his touch gentle, cautious, as he examined the wound.

She tried to focus on anything else, on the landscape around them, the faint rustle of leaves in the wind, the cool mountain air against her skin. But her gaze drifted back to him, to the focused intensity in his eyes, the careful precision in his movements as he tended to her wound, his hand lingering on her arm a moment longer than necessary.

"There," he said softly, his voice barely more than a murmur. "That should help, for now."

Rebecca felt a faint, ironic smile tug at her lips as she looked up at him, her voice edged with dry amusement. "So, what is this, Captain Jarred? You taking care of me, or just hoping I don't die on you?"

He looked at her, his gaze softening, a flicker of warmth and something else she couldn't quite name lingering in his eyes. For a moment, he didn't answer, his expression unreadable, as though he were weighing his words.

"Maybe a little of both," he replied, his voice low, rough with unspoken emotion. "Just... try not to make this any harder than it already is."

She gave a short laugh, though the sound was weak, edged with the remnants of pain. "Trust me, I'm not exactly loving the idea of becoming dead weight."

He didn't respond, but his hand lingered on hers, a subtle, quiet assurance that left her feeling strangely comforted, despite the exhaustion that pulled at her, the pain that dulled her senses. She closed her eyes, letting herself sink into the moment, feeling the steady warmth of his hand, the grounding presence of his touch.

They sat in silence, the air around them still, heavy with unspoken words, a fragile truce that neither of them dared disturb. Rebecca felt her strength slipping, her body finally surrendering to the fatigue that had been building since the moment they'd started this journey. She fought to stay awake, but the comfort of his presence, the quiet, unspoken promise in his touch, was enough to let her guard down, if only for a moment.

Nolan stayed beside her, his gaze fixed on her, a quiet intensity in his eyes as he watched her drift off. And for the first time, she felt truly safe, a feeling she hadn't thought possible in this world, in the midst of the chaos and danger that had become their reality.

As sleep finally claimed her, her last thought was of him, of the quiet, unyielding strength that had become her anchor, her lifeline in this dark, uncertain world.

Chapter 12: "Unspoken Truce"

The sky was darkening as they stumbled into the remains of the old church, its roof half-collapsed and its walls scarred by time and war. Broken shards of stained glass littered the floor, casting fractured colors across the crumbling pews, remnants of a beauty that had been long forgotten in this new world. Rebecca felt a strange sense of reverence as she crossed the threshold, her steps echoing softly in the hollow silence.

Nolan followed close behind, his gaze sweeping the space, his posture tense even in the face of exhaustion. They'd been walking for hours, every step a reminder of their injuries, their shared weariness. The mission and Miguel's betrayal still weighed heavily between them, but for now, it was all they could do to survive the night.

Rebecca sank onto one of the remaining pews, barely holding back a wince as she eased herself down, her injured side flaring in protest. She pressed a hand to her ribs, biting back the pain, but Nolan noticed, his gaze narrowing as he approached her, crossing his arms with a look that managed to convey both exasperation and worry.

"Doctor Adams," he drawled, his tone thick with sarcasm. "Should I remind you that sitting still and bleeding isn't exactly the best survival tactic?"

She shot him a look, though the effort was somewhat diminished by her obvious discomfort. "I'm fine, Captain Jarred. Unless you're planning to lecture me on my chosen sitting position?"

Nolan's mouth twitched, though he didn't give her the satisfaction of a full smile. "I'd consider it if I thought you'd actually listen."

He sank down beside her, his body tense, his expression grim as he studied the injury beneath her jacket. She felt a prickling sense of irritation, a stubborn urge to tell him to mind his own business, but the look in his eyes—a quiet, restrained concern—held her tongue.

"Hold still," he muttered, reaching into his pack for the last of their supplies. He pulled out a strip of cloth, his fingers steady as he carefully pressed it against her side, his touch firm but gentle.

Rebecca's breath hitched as his hand lingered, the warmth of his skin seeping through the cloth, grounding her in a way that made her acutely aware of their closeness. She looked away, fighting the rush of heat that crept up her neck, a traitorous flush that she could only hope he hadn't noticed.

"Always the hero, aren't you?" she murmured, her voice laced with irony, a weak attempt to deflect from the intensity of the moment.

Nolan's eyes flicked up, meeting hers with a look that was both amused and exasperated. "If I'm the hero, Doc, I'd hate to meet the villain." He pressed down a little harder, and she barely held back a wince.

"Funny," she replied, her tone edged with sarcasm. "I didn't realize 'pain management' was part of your treatment plan."

He chuckled, the sound low and warm, a surprising contrast to the tension in the air. "Hey, pain means you're still alive. Think of it as a gift."

"Oh, how generous of you," she muttered, though the faint, reluctant smile on her lips betrayed her irritation.

They fell into a charged silence, the weight of the day settling over them as the last of the light faded, casting the church into shadows. The only sounds were their breathing and the soft rustle of fabric as he finished tying off the makeshift bandage, his fingers lingering on her arm a moment longer than necessary.

Rebecca felt her heart quicken, a quiet thrill that sent a shiver through her. She met his gaze, the unspoken tension between them flaring, a spark igniting in the dim light. He was close, too close, and yet... she couldn't bring herself to pull away.

Nolan's expression softened, his eyes tracing over her face with an intensity that left her breathless, his hand hovering near her cheek, as if he were trying to decide whether to close the distance. She swallowed, the silence thickening, her pulse pounding as she felt the steady warmth of his hand resting against her arm.

"You're a difficult woman to keep alive, Doc," he murmured, his voice rough, edged with a tension that was as much frustration as it was something else.

"Good thing you like a challenge," she replied, her voice barely above a whisper, the irony there a feeble shield against the raw vulnerability she felt, the way his presence seemed to seep into her, warming her in a way that left her feeling exposed, unsteady.

He let out a soft, humorless laugh, his gaze intense, unwavering. "You really think that's why I'm here?"

Her heart skipped, a flicker of something unspoken passing between them, something she couldn't ignore, no matter how hard she tried. The weight of the moment settled over them, a fragile, charged intimacy that felt both exhilarating and terrifying.

Rebecca's breath caught as he leaned closer, his hand sliding up to cup her cheek, his thumb brushing against her skin in a touch that was both gentle and possessive. She closed her eyes, the heat of his hand seeping into her, grounding her, a quiet, unspoken assurance that, in this moment, she wasn't alone.

And then, before she could second-guess herself, before she could let the weight of everything between them hold her back, she leaned in, her lips finding his in a kiss that was soft, hesitant, yet laced with a desperation that she hadn't realized she was carrying.

Nolan didn't pull back; if anything, he seemed to lean into her, his hand sliding to the back of her neck, pulling her closer, deepening the kiss with a fierceness that left her breathless. She felt his other hand at her waist, steadying her, anchoring her in a way that felt both dangerous and right.

The world around them faded, leaving only the press of his lips, the warmth of his body against hers, the steady, grounding presence that she hadn't realized she needed. Each touch, each kiss felt like a fragile, desperate plea, a quiet acknowledgment of the loneliness they'd both been carrying, the unspoken ache that had simmered between them since the beginning.

When they finally pulled apart, their breaths mingling in the cool, empty air, they looked at each other, a quiet wonderment lingering in their gazes, as though they were both surprised by the depth of the moment they'd shared.

Rebecca let out a soft, ironic laugh, her voice shaking with a mix of relief and disbelief. "So... do we pretend that didn't just happen?"

Nolan's mouth quirked into a faint, reluctant smile, his gaze softening as he reached up, brushing a strand of hair away from her face. "Good luck with that, Doc," he murmured, his voice laced with irony. "Not sure it's that easy to forget."

She smiled, though the ache in her chest, the quiet, vulnerable thrill that lingered, left her feeling unsteady, as though the ground beneath her feet had shifted in ways she hadn't anticipated.

They settled into a comfortable silence, their hands still entwined, as though neither of them could bring themselves to pull away, despite the unspoken tension that lingered between them, the quiet, fragile understanding that this was more than just a moment, more than just a passing connection.

And as they sat there in the dim light of the ruined church, the shadows thickening around them, Rebecca felt a quiet certainty settle over her, a realization that, no matter what came next, no matter what the world threw at them, they would face it together.

But neither of them spoke of it. Neither of them dared put words to the quiet, unspoken bond they'd discovered in the heart of the chaos, knowing that, for now, it was enough to simply be, to share this moment, this fleeting intimacy, as the world outside faded away.

Chapter 13: "Estrangement"

Morning broke with the first light filtering through the shattered remains of the church windows, casting pale, fractured beams over the worn stone floor. Nolan stood near the doorway, his gaze fixed on the dim landscape outside, his posture tense, closed off, like a barrier she wasn't meant to cross. Rebecca watched him from where she sat, her arms crossed, her thoughts racing.

The chill of the dawn crept through the cracks in the walls, but she couldn't shake the colder sensation of being shut out, the stark difference between last night's closeness and this morning's calculated distance. She drew in a slow, steadying breath, trying to reconcile the memories of his tenderness with the guarded, aloof figure now standing before her.

At last, she rose, her steps echoing softly as she crossed the space between them, her voice steady though her heart was anything but. "So," she began, keeping her tone light, edged with forced calm, "is this how it's going to be?"

He didn't look at her, his jaw tightening as he shifted his weight, every line of his body radiating discomfort. "I don't know what you're talking about," he replied, his voice clipped, dismissive.

Rebecca clenched her fists, feeling a flare of irritation that quickly smothered any lingering warmth from the night before. "Really?" she said, sarcasm lacing her words. "You don't think maybe there's something to discuss? Something a little more complicated than just pretending last night didn't happen?"

His jaw clenched, his gaze fixed firmly on a distant point beyond the broken window. "It's better this way," he said quietly, his voice low, almost cold. "Better to keep things simple."

Rebecca felt a flash of anger, hot and sharp, slicing through the hurt that had settled in her chest. "Simple?" she repeated, her tone incredulous. "That's what you call this? You think you can just put walls back up and pretend nothing happened?"

Nolan's gaze flicked to her, a shadow passing over his eyes, but he held his ground, his expression hardened, impassive. "Last night was... a mistake," he said, each word carefully chosen, as though hoping the detachment would smother whatever lay beneath.

The bluntness of it hit her like a slap, a surge of hurt tightening her throat, but she forced herself to hold her composure, to keep her voice steady, if only for her own dignity. "A mistake," she echoed, her tone icy, though her heart twisted with each word. "Well, that's a relief. Wouldn't want to think you actually meant any of it."

He looked away, his shoulders tensing, his hands clenching at his sides as though he were physically restraining himself. "Rebecca, I told you," he said, his voice rough, edged with a frustration that seemed to mirror her own. "I'm not someone you want to get involved with."

"Funny," she shot back, her sarcasm sharper now, her voice laced with anger. "Because last night, you seemed pretty involved."

The words hung in the air, the charged silence stretching between them, thick and suffocating. Rebecca searched his face, looking for any sign of the man who'd held her so tenderly just hours before, the man who'd made her feel safe in a way she hadn't felt in years.

But all she saw was the closed-off, guarded figure he was so determined to be, as though he'd built a fortress around himself overnight, barring her from even the faintest hint of vulnerability.

"Fine," she said, crossing her arms, her tone brittle with defiance. "If that's how you want it, Nolan. If that's what you're so terrified of—"

"It's not about fear," he snapped, his voice sharper than she'd ever heard it, raw with an edge that surprised them both. He clenched his jaw, looking away, his gaze darkening as he struggled with words that seemed to weigh more than she could understand. "It's... it's not something you would understand."

Rebecca felt her anger flare again, her irritation spilling over in a quiet, biting laugh. "Try me," she challenged, her eyes narrowing. "Because from where I'm standing, it looks an awful lot like fear."

He took a step closer, his gaze flashing with a mixture of frustration and something darker, something haunted that she couldn't quite name. "You don't know what I've been through, Rebecca," he said, his voice low, rough. "You don't know the kind of life I've led—the kind of things I've lost."

The words fell like stones between them, a hint of something she'd only glimpsed in rare moments, something he'd buried deep beneath his stoic exterior. She could see it now, a flicker of pain, raw and jagged, that he tried so desperately to hide, to lock away.

Rebecca's breath caught, her anger softening, replaced by a quiet, aching understanding. She held his gaze, her voice softening, though the sarcasm remained. "And so what?" she asked, crossing her arms, tilting her head. "That means you just get to push me away? Pretend like you're the only one who's ever been hurt?"

He didn't answer, but his expression shifted, his gaze flickering with something vulnerable, something raw that he couldn't fully hide. She could see it in his eyes, the weight of whatever haunted him, the wounds he carried that refused to heal.

"Nolan," she said quietly, taking a step closer, her voice softened but still edged with defiance. "If you think that hiding behind walls and pushing people away is going to keep you safe, then you're lying to yourself. You're just scared, even if you can't admit it."

He let out a short, bitter laugh, shaking his head as though he couldn't quite believe her words. "You think it's that simple?"

"Simple?" she repeated, her tone a mix of incredulity and irritation. "Believe me, Nolan, I think you've made it plenty complicated."

A bitter silence settled over them, the air thick with the weight of everything they weren't saying, everything that hung between them like a fragile, fractured thread. Rebecca felt the frustration, the hurt simmering beneath the surface, a resentment that she couldn't fully express, even as she looked at him with a defiance she hadn't felt before.

"So this is it, then?" she said, her voice tight, each word carefully controlled. "You're just going to shut down, go back to playing the tough, untouchable soldier?"

His gaze hardened, his jaw clenched as he met her challenge with a look that was both frustrated and resigned. "Rebecca—"

But before he could finish, she cut him off, her voice sharp with irony. "Because let me tell you, Nolan, for someone who's so afraid of getting close, you have a really strange way of showing it."

The words hung in the air, and for a moment, he looked at her, truly looked at her, as though the weight of her accusation had struck something deep within him, something he couldn't ignore. His gaze softened, just a fraction, a flicker of regret flashing across his face before he quickly buried it.

She saw it, that unguarded moment, that hint of vulnerability he tried so desperately to hide. And though the anger still simmered within her, though the frustration still burned, she couldn't ignore the quiet ache that settled in her chest, the realization that, perhaps, he was just as lost as she was.

But neither of them spoke. The words, the anger, the hurt—all of it lingered between them, unspoken, unresolved, a silent, fragile truce that neither of them dared to break.

Chapter 14: "Duty vs. Desire"

The sun was setting by the time they stumbled upon the camp—a small, ramshackle gathering of tents and makeshift shelters set against the rocky edge of a dried-out riverbed. The landscape was bleak, dotted with patches of dry grass and half-dead shrubs, the remnants of a world that had once thrived. But to Rebecca, the sight was both welcome and disquieting. They'd been on the run for so long that even the semblance of civilization felt foreign, almost threatening in its familiarity.

Nolan tensed beside her, his gaze sweeping the camp, his hand hovering near his weapon as though he expected an attack at any moment. "You sure about this?" he asked, his voice low, edged with suspicion.

Rebecca let out a breath she hadn't realized she'd been holding. "We don't have much choice," she replied, her voice equally tense. "We need supplies, and unless you're planning on surviving on pure attitude, we're going to need their help."

Nolan gave a short, humorless laugh. "Attitude's gotten me this far, hasn't it?"

She shot him a look, crossing her arms as they waited just outside the camp's perimeter. "If you want to try winning them over with your sparkling personality, be my guest."

A faint smirk tugged at his lips, though his expression remained guarded. "Let's just get what we need and get out."

They approached the camp cautiously, their presence quickly noticed by a few members of the group. Eyes turned their way, weary faces lined with exhaustion and suspicion as the survivors took in the sight of two strangers, their appearances marked by the hardship of the road. An older man approached them, his gaze cautious, his posture wary as he sized them up.

"Who are you?" he demanded, his tone brusque, though there was a hint of desperation in his voice.

Nolan stepped forward, his expression hardening. "We're just passing through," he said simply, his voice steady. "Looking to trade, if you've got anything to spare."

The man's gaze flickered between them, his eyes narrowing as he took in Rebecca's worn clothes, the faint traces of exhaustion etched into her face. "And her?" he asked, his tone laced with suspicion.

Rebecca felt a prickle of unease, but she forced herself to hold his gaze, her posture steady. "Just trying to survive, like everyone else," she replied, her voice calm, though her heart raced.

But before she could say more, a woman stepped forward, her eyes widening as they landed on Rebecca's face. She clutched at the arm of the man beside her, her voice trembling with a mixture of shock and recognition.

"It's her," the woman whispered, her gaze fixed on Rebecca. "She's the one... the doctor. The one who... made the vaccine."

The words hung in the air, a ripple of realization spreading through the group as they turned to look at her, their eyes widening with a mixture of hope and fear. Rebecca felt the weight of their gaze, the sudden intensity of their scrutiny pressing down on her, suffocating in its expectation.

Nolan shifted beside her, his posture tensing, his gaze flickering over the crowd with a growing wariness. "Time to go," he muttered, his voice barely above a whisper, his hand reaching for her arm to pull her back.

But before they could turn, a man stepped forward, his expression wild, desperate, his voice shaking as he reached out toward her. "Please," he begged, his eyes wide, filled with a desperation that bordered on madness. "You... you can save us. You have to help us."

Rebecca felt a pang of sympathy, the weight of his desperation settling over her like a heavy, suffocating blanket. "I... I don't have enough," she began, her voice hesitant, though the words felt hollow in her throat. "The vaccine isn't... it's not ready."

The man's face contorted, a flash of anger mingling with the desperation in his gaze. "You're lying," he hissed, his voice laced with accusation. "You just want to keep it for yourself."

The accusation hit her like a blow, the anger, the betrayal in his eyes cutting through her defenses. She took a step back, her heart racing, but Nolan stepped in front of her, his stance protective, his gaze hard as he fixed his eyes on the man.

"Back off," he said, his voice cold, edged with a warning that left no room for argument. "She doesn't owe you anything."

The man's gaze flickered to Nolan, his anger flaring, his hands clenched into fists as he glared at him, the desperation in his eyes darkening, hardening into something far more dangerous. "You don't understand," he spat, his voice rising. "She has the cure. She has the power to save us, and she's keeping it to herself."

A murmur of agreement rippled through the crowd, the faces around them hardening, their eyes filling with a mixture of anger and desperation as they turned on her, their voices rising in accusation, in resentment.

Rebecca felt her heart pound, the weight of their anger, their fear pressing down on her, suffocating in its intensity. She looked to Nolan, her eyes wide, her breath catching as the crowd began to close in around them, their voices growing louder, more insistent.

"Enough!" Nolan's voice cut through the chaos, sharp and unyielding, a note of authority that silenced the crowd, if only for a moment. He stepped forward, his gaze hard, his posture commanding as he faced them, his voice cold, edged with a fierce protectiveness that sent a shiver through her.

"She's not here to save anyone," he said, his voice steady, unyielding. "And she doesn't owe any of you her life. If you want to survive, find another way. But stay back. Now."

The crowd hesitated, the weight of his words settling over them, the anger in their eyes tempered by a flicker of fear as they took in his stance, the hardness in his gaze, the authority in his voice.

But even as the crowd began to disperse, Rebecca could feel the weight of their anger, their resentment lingering in the air, a dark, oppressive presence that pressed down on her, heavy and unrelenting.

She looked up at Nolan, her breath shaky, a faint, grateful smile tugging at her lips despite the tension that lingered between them. "Thank you," she murmured, her voice barely more than a whisper, though the gratitude in her gaze was unmistakable.

Nolan scoffed, his expression unreadable as he looked away, his tone laced with sarcasm. "Just doing my job, Doc," he replied, his voice cool, detached, though there was a flicker of something unspoken in his gaze.

Rebecca raised an eyebrow, a faint, knowing smile tugging at her lips. "Oh, of course. Just a job. Nothing personal."

He gave her a look, somewhere between exasperation and irritation, though there was a warmth in his gaze, a softness that he couldn't quite hide. "Keep smiling like that, and you're going to ruin my reputation."

She let out a soft, ironic laugh, crossing her arms as she looked at him, her gaze filled with a quiet, knowing amusement. "You're doing a pretty good job of that yourself, Captain."

He shook his head, though she caught the faintest hint of a smile, a reluctant, fleeting warmth that softened the tension between them, if only for a moment. But even as the silence settled over them, the weight of the unspoken lingered, the quiet, fragile bond that bound them together growing stronger, even as they both fought to ignore it.

Chapter 15: "Taken"

The evening air was heavy, thick with an unnatural silence that had settled over the camp like a warning. Rebecca's instincts were on high alert, though she couldn't say precisely what had triggered them—maybe it was the way the light was dying faster than usual, casting everything in shadow, or the way even the sounds of the night seemed to fade into the background. But whatever it was, it filled her with a mounting unease.

Nolan moved through the camp, checking the perimeter with his usual sharp, careful gaze, his hand never far from his weapon. They'd both grown accustomed to danger, to the constant feeling of being hunted, but this felt different—darker, more imminent, as though something was lurking just beyond the edge of their awareness, waiting for the perfect moment to strike.

Rebecca stood at the edge of their makeshift tent, her eyes scanning the trees, her heart pounding in a rhythm she couldn't quite calm. She glanced over her shoulder, her gaze landing on Nolan's shadowy form as he moved through the camp, his posture tense, his focus unyielding.

Then, as if out of nowhere, the darkness broke, a sudden rush of movement filling the camp as shadows emerged from the trees, silent and deadly. Before she could even scream, hands were on her, rough and unyielding, dragging her back into the woods as she fought against them, her voice muffled, her struggles met with a cruel, mocking laughter.

She caught a glimpse of Nolan's face as he turned, his eyes widening with a mixture of horror and fury as he saw her being dragged away. He moved to intercept them, his hand reaching for his weapon, but he was outnumbered, the camp flooded with figures dressed in dark, combat-ready gear, their faces hidden beneath masks.

"Run!" Rebecca managed to scream, her voice hoarse, desperate, but it was too late. The last thing she saw before darkness enveloped her was Nolan's furious gaze, his face twisted with a mixture of anger and determination that sent a shiver down her spine.

When she awoke, the world was dark and silent, the faint hum of generators and the distant echo of voices filling her ears as she blinked, disoriented, her head pounding with a dull, persistent ache. She was in a small, dimly lit room, the walls lined with metal, the air thick with a sterile, cold scent that sent a shiver down her spine.

She struggled against the ropes that bound her wrists, her mind racing as she tried to piece together what had happened. The last thing she remembered was Nolan's face, the look of desperation in his eyes as he'd tried to reach her.

The door creaked open, and she tensed, her heart pounding as a figure stepped inside, his face obscured by the shadows. But as he moved into the light, a chill ran down her spine, her breath catching as she recognized him.

Lucifer.

He was taller than she'd expected, his presence commanding, his expression a mixture of charm and malice as he looked at her, his gaze tracing over her with a calculated intensity that left her feeling exposed, vulnerable.

"Well, well," he murmured, his voice low, smooth, laced with a dark amusement that sent a chill through her. "The famous Dr. Adams. I must say, you're even more intriguing in person."

Rebecca met his gaze, forcing herself to hold steady, her voice cold, defiant. "If you think you can intimidate me, you're going to be disappointed."

Lucifer chuckled, a low, mocking sound that echoed through the room, his gaze filled with a twisted admiration that was as unsettling as it was infuriating. "Oh, I don't need to intimidate you, Dr. Adams," he replied, his voice laced with a chilling calm. "I just need you to listen."

She glared at him, her hands clenching against the ropes that bound her, her breath steady, even as her heart raced. "I'm not interested in anything you have to say."

"Ah, but that's where you're wrong," he said, his tone soft, almost coaxing. "You see, Dr. Adams, we're not so different, you and I. We both want the same thing—survival. A new beginning, free from the shackles of the past."

She felt a surge of anger, her voice hardening as she met his gaze. "Don't you dare compare us. I'm nothing like you."

He smiled, a faint, amused glint in his eyes. "Aren't you?" he murmured, his voice soft, insidious. "You created the vaccine, after all. The power to shape the future, to decide who lives and who dies—that's not something you can take lightly, Dr. Adams. And whether you like it or not, that power makes you more like me than you're willing to admit."

Rebecca felt a shiver run down her spine, his words digging into her like barbs, sharp and unyielding. She clenched her jaw, refusing to let him see the effect he was having on her, the way his words sent a chill of fear and revulsion through her.

"I created the vaccine to save people," she said, her voice steady, though the anger simmered beneath the surface. "Not to control them."

Lucifer's smile widened, his gaze filled with a dark, twisted amusement. "Is that what you tell yourself? That you're a savior? A hero?" He leaned closer, his voice dropping to a whisper. "Tell me,

Dr. Adams, how many lives have you saved? And how many have you condemned?"

She felt her heart race, his words cutting through her defenses, a flicker of doubt settling over her as she met his gaze, her voice faltering. "I... I did what I had to do."

He nodded, a faint, mocking smile on his lips. "Of course you did. And now, with that vaccine, you hold the fate of humanity in your hands. Imagine the possibilities, Dr. Adams. Imagine what we could accomplish together."

Rebecca felt a surge of revulsion, her voice hardening as she met his gaze. "I'd rather die than work with you."

Lucifer's expression softened, his gaze filled with a twisted sympathy that was as unsettling as it was infuriating. "Oh, Dr. Adams," he murmured, his voice low, almost gentle. "Don't be so quick to dismiss me. You'd be surprised how many people have said the same thing... and changed their minds."

She glared at him, her body tense, every muscle coiled with anger, with defiance. "Whatever you're planning, it won't work. I won't help you, and I won't let you use the vaccine for your own twisted goals."

He chuckled, a faint, amused sound, his gaze filled with a dark, calculating intensity. "I wouldn't be so sure, Dr. Adams. After all, everyone has a price. Even you."

She felt a surge of anger, her voice sharp, defiant. "And you'll never know what mine is."

He smiled, a faint, amused glint in his eyes. "Oh, I think I already do."

The door opened, and he stepped back, his gaze lingering on her for a moment before he turned, his voice laced with a quiet, chilling calm. "I'll give you some time to think it over, Dr. Adams. But remember, the clock is ticking. And every second you waste... someone else pays the price."

With that, he turned and left, the door closing behind him with a soft, ominous click, leaving her alone in the dim, suffocating silence.

In the dark, Rebecca's mind raced, her heart pounding as she tried to process his words, the weight of his twisted vision pressing down on her, suffocating in its intensity. She forced herself to take a deep breath, her gaze fixed on the door, the faint, stubborn hope that somewhere, somehow, Nolan was coming for her.

Nolan.

The thought of him sent a rush of warmth through her, a flicker of strength that she clung to, even as doubt and fear threatened to overwhelm her. She could still see his face, the determination in his eyes, the fierce protectiveness that had become her lifeline, her anchor.

She closed her eyes, the image of him steadying her, grounding her as she waited, her heart pounding with a quiet, unyielding hope that he would come for her, that he wouldn't let her face this alone.

Chapter 16: "Escape Plan"

The darkness in Lucifer's camp was thick and oppressive, broken only by the occasional flicker of firelight casting strange shadows over the bleak, metal structures. Nolan moved through the shadows with practiced ease, his steps silent, his gaze sharp and unyielding. Every muscle was tensed, every nerve on high alert as he navigated the twisted maze of guards and hunters that patrolled the area, their footsteps echoing through the stillness.

He'd been planning this for hours, every step, every calculated risk, every careful maneuver designed to bring him closer to Rebecca. The thought of her, trapped somewhere in the heart of Lucifer's twisted domain, filled him with a cold, determined fury that drowned out any fear or hesitation. He wouldn't leave without her.

Slipping into the shadows, he spotted the narrow, unguarded side entrance he'd observed from the outer perimeter. It was tucked away behind a pile of crates, half-hidden in darkness, and just the kind of overlooked access point he could use to his advantage.

With one last glance around to ensure he was alone, he slid through the door, his body tensed, ready for anything. The corridor was narrow, poorly lit, the metal walls echoing his soft footsteps as he moved deeper into the complex, his senses on high alert. He had no map, no clear direction, but he knew he was getting closer—the silence, the stillness, the faint, lingering scent of antiseptic and iron told him he was on the right path.

And then, through the dim light, he saw her.

Rebecca was seated on a metal chair, her hands bound in front of her, her face illuminated by a single, flickering light above. Her gaze was fixed on the floor, her expression hard, focused, though there was a faint weariness in her eyes that cut through him like a knife.

He stepped into the room, his voice low, barely more than a whisper. "Rebecca."

She looked up, her eyes widening with a mixture of relief and disbelief as she took him in. "Nolan," she breathed, her voice filled with a quiet, desperate hope that sent a surge of determination through him. "How did you...?"

He moved to her side, his hands already working on the ropes that bound her wrists. "You didn't really think I'd leave you here, did you?" he murmured, his tone laced with a faint, teasing sarcasm that belied the intensity of his focus.

She shot him a look, a faint smile tugging at her lips despite the situation. "I didn't think you'd get caught in the first place."

"Touché," he replied, though his gaze softened as he looked at her, his fingers lingering on her wrists as he freed her, his touch warm, grounding. "Are you alright?"

She nodded, though the weariness was evident in her eyes, the faint shadows underlining her exhaustion. "I'm fine," she said, her voice steady, though there was a flicker of vulnerability that she couldn't quite hide. "But we need to get out of here."

Nolan's gaze hardened, his expression fierce as he nodded. "I've got a way out, but we'll have to move fast. This place is crawling with hunters."

Rebecca stood, testing her strength as she flexed her wrists, her gaze fixed on him with a mixture of gratitude and defiance. "I can handle it," she said, her voice firm, though there was a faint edge of irritation in her tone that didn't escape his notice.

He raised an eyebrow, his tone laced with sarcasm. "Oh, I'm sure. You seem to have done a great job of that so far."

She shot him a look, her eyes flashing with irritation. "And you're just full of humility, aren't you?"

"Just trying to keep things realistic," he replied, though there was a faint smirk on his lips as he met her gaze. "Now let's move before they notice you're gone."

They slipped through the dimly lit corridors, their footsteps soft, their movements precise as they navigated the labyrinthine passages of Lucifer's camp. The silence was thick, oppressive, the only sounds the faint echo of footsteps, the distant murmur of voices. Every turn, every shadow felt like a threat, a danger waiting to pounce, but they moved together, their steps in sync, their focus sharp.

At one point, they heard the low murmur of approaching voices, the unmistakable sound of hunters moving through the corridor. Nolan held up a hand, signaling her to stop, his gaze intense as he scanned the area for a hiding spot. Spotting a narrow alcove in the wall, he pulled her into it, his body pressed close to hers as they stood in the shadows, their breaths shallow, their eyes locked.

The voices grew louder, the footsteps drawing closer, and Rebecca felt her pulse quicken, her heart pounding as she looked up at Nolan, his face mere inches from hers, his gaze steady, focused. The tension between them was thick, electric, an unspoken understanding passing between them, a silent acknowledgement of the danger, the closeness, the trust they'd built.

Her breath hitched, her gaze dropping to his lips, the faint flicker of emotion in his eyes sending a thrill through her that she couldn't quite suppress. She felt the warmth of his body, the steady strength of his presence grounding her, steadying her in a way that was both comforting and exhilarating.

Nolan's gaze softened, his hand resting lightly on her arm, his thumb brushing against her skin in a way that felt both possessive and gentle. And before she could second-guess herself, before she could let the weight of their circumstances hold her back, she leaned in, her lips finding his in a kiss that was fierce, desperate, a quiet, unspoken plea.

He didn't pull back; instead, he met her kiss with an intensity that left her breathless, his hands sliding up to cup her face, pulling her closer, deepening the kiss with a fervor that spoke of all the things they couldn't say, the emotions they couldn't express. The world around them faded, leaving only the warmth of his touch, the steady, grounding presence that had become her anchor.

When they finally pulled back, their breaths mingling in the dim, heavy air, they looked at each other, a quiet, unspoken understanding passing between them. But neither of them spoke, the weight of the moment settling over them as they turned, slipping back into the shadows, their focus returning to the task at hand.

They navigated the maze of corridors, their movements swift, silent, their senses honed to every flicker of light, every murmur of sound. The tension between them was thick, but they didn't speak, each of them focused, driven by the shared goal of escape, of survival.

As they reached the outer perimeter, Nolan paused, his gaze fixed on the last line of guards that stood between them and freedom. He turned to her, his expression hard, determined, his voice barely more than a whisper. "Stay close. We're almost there."

Rebecca nodded, her gaze steady, her voice calm, though her heart raced with a mixture of fear and exhilaration. "Lead the way, Captain."

They slipped through the shadows, their movements precise, calculated, each step a delicate dance of survival. But as they moved, she felt a surge of gratitude, a quiet, fierce determination that matched his own, the knowledge that, together, they were stronger, more unbreakable than she'd ever thought possible.

And as they finally reached the edge of the camp, slipping into the cover of the trees, Rebecca felt a quiet, unspoken promise settle over her, a certainty that, no matter what came next, they would face it together.

Chapter 17: "On the Edge"

The night was pitch-black, the heavy clouds swallowing what little moonlight filtered through the trees, casting the forest into an oppressive darkness. Nolan moved through the dense underbrush, his steps quick and silent as he adjusted his grip on Rebecca, her body limp in his arms. The wound on her side was still bleeding, the dark stain of blood spreading across her clothes, but she was breathing, her shallow breaths warm against his neck.

He kept his gaze fixed on the path ahead, his mind racing as he calculated each step, every turn, every shadow that seemed to shift and move in the darkness. They didn't have much time. The infected were closing in behind them, drawn to the scent of blood, to the faint, muffled sounds of their escape.

A faint groan escaped her lips, a quiet sound that sent a jolt of relief through him, even as it reminded him of the fragility of their situation. She was still with him, still holding on. But for how long?

"Rebecca," he murmured, his voice low, steady, his gaze flicking down to her face. "You're going to be alright, you hear me?"

Her eyelids fluttered, her gaze unfocused as she looked up at him, her expression dazed, but there was a faint, wry smile on her lips that managed to convey both irritation and humor even in her weakened state.

"Well," she whispered, her voice barely more than a rasp, "aren't you the optimist."

He huffed, though his expression softened as he looked down at her, his grip tightening. "You can complain all you want once we're out of here, Doc. Until then, try to stay conscious."

She let out a faint, shaky laugh, though the sound was laced with pain, her face contorted in a grimace as he shifted her weight, her hand clutching weakly at his shoulder. "Bossy as ever, I see," she murmured, her gaze flickering with a faint glint of humor, though her voice was weak, strained.

He didn't answer, but his grip tightened, his jaw set with a grim determination as he continued forward, his gaze flicking over the path ahead, his senses honed to every shift in the shadows, every whisper of sound that seemed to grow louder with each passing moment.

And then, through the trees, he caught a glimpse of movement, a flicker of pale, rotting flesh illuminated by a shaft of moonlight. The infected. They were close, too close, their hollow, rasping breaths filling the air as they moved through the forest, their steps slow but relentless, drawn to the scent of blood, to the faint traces of life that lingered in the night.

Nolan felt his pulse quicken, his mind racing as he calculated his options, the risks, the chances of escape. They couldn't outrun them—not with Rebecca injured, her strength fading with every step. He'd have to fight, to hold them off long enough to get her to safety.

"Stay with me," he murmured, his voice barely more than a whisper as he lowered her to the ground, his gaze fixed on the infected that crept closer, their hollow eyes fixed on him with a hunger that sent a shiver down his spine.

Rebecca looked up at him, her eyes glassy, her expression hazy with pain, but there was a faint flicker of understanding in her gaze, a quiet determination that matched his own. "You're... not leaving me, are you?" she murmured, her voice barely more than a rasp.

He looked down at her, his expression fierce, his gaze steady as he met her eyes. "Not a chance."

She gave him a faint, wry smile, though her gaze softened, her voice barely more than a whisper. "Good," she murmured, her fingers brushing against his hand, her touch light, fleeting, but warm.

He didn't let go, his hand steady against hers as he drew his weapon, his gaze fixed on the approaching figures, his body tensed, ready to strike. The infected stumbled forward, their eyes empty, hollow, their movements slow but unyielding as they closed in, their breaths rattling in the cold night air.

The first one lunged at him, its mouth open, its eyes blank, but he met its attack with a swift, calculated blow, his movements precise, efficient. He took down the next with a quick, clean shot, his hand steady, his mind focused, his only thought to protect her, to keep her safe.

When the last of them fell, he turned back to her, his breath heavy, his gaze fierce as he knelt beside her, his hand steady as he touched her face, his voice low, steady. "Rebecca. Can you hear me?"

She looked up at him, her gaze unfocused, her expression hazy, but there was a faint, stubborn glint in her eyes, a quiet strength that defied the pain that gripped her. "Still here," she murmured, her voice weak but steady, her fingers brushing against his hand, her touch light, warm.

He let out a faint, relieved breath, his grip tightening on her hand as he looked down at her, his gaze softening, a flicker of something unspoken lingering in his eyes. "Good. Because I'm not done carrying you out of here."

She managed a faint smile, though her gaze softened, her voice barely more than a whisper. "You know... I always thought... you were just a little too sure of yourself."

He huffed, though there was a faint, amused glint in his eyes as he looked down at her. "Is that so?"

She gave a faint nod, her gaze flickering with a hint of humor, though her voice was weak, her breaths shallow. "Yeah... always thought... you were just a little too... invincible."

He didn't answer, his hand steady against hers as he lifted her once more, his gaze fixed on the path ahead, his mind focused, determined.

But her voice, soft and unsteady, broke through his focus, her words barely more than a whisper.

"Nolan," she murmured, her voice weak, faltering, but filled with a quiet, desperate sincerity. "I know... you probably don't want to hear this, but... you're more than just... more than just some protector to me."

He looked down at her, his expression hardening, his gaze fierce, but he didn't speak, his hand steady as he held hers, his touch warm, grounding. Her words hung between them, a quiet, unspoken confession that lingered in the cold night air, fragile and precious, but he didn't answer, didn't dare to break the silence.

Rebecca looked up at him, her gaze soft, her voice barely more than a whisper. "Don't... don't you have anything to say to that?"

He held her gaze, his expression unyielding, his grip on her hand firm, but he remained silent, his gaze steady, filled with a quiet, fierce protectiveness that spoke louder than any words. And in that moment, as the silence settled over them, she felt a quiet, unspoken understanding pass between them, a silent, fragile promise that he would be there, no matter what came next.

Chapter 18: "Echoes of the Past"

They stumbled into the abandoned cabin just as night swallowed the forest, the air inside thick with the smell of old wood and dust. It was a modest structure, worn but stable, the faint remnants of a once-cozy home still visible in the faint glow of the moon that seeped through the cracks in the walls. It wasn't much, but after the brutal hours they'd spent on the run, it felt like a sanctuary.

Nolan set Rebecca down gently on an old, faded couch, his movements slow and careful as he adjusted her, his gaze flickering with concern as he took in her pale face, the exhaustion etched into every line of her expression.

"Comfortable?" he asked, his tone laced with his usual dry sarcasm, though there was a warmth in his eyes that softened the edge.

She gave him a faint smile, though the effort was clearly taxing. "I've had worse. At least this place isn't actively trying to kill me."

"High standards, Doc. I'll make a note of that for next time."

She let out a soft laugh, her eyes closing as she leaned back, her breath steadying, her body relaxing for the first time in what felt like days. Silence settled over them, a quiet, fragile peace that felt both comforting and unsettling, as though the cabin itself were holding its breath, waiting.

Nolan moved to the fireplace, gathering what little wood was left, his hands steady, his gaze distant as he worked. The silence was thick, heavy with unspoken words, with memories that lingered in the shadows, waiting to be unearthed. And as he worked, Rebecca watched him, her gaze tracing the lines of his face, the tension in his jaw, the weariness in his eyes.

She'd seen him in so many different states—angry, determined, vulnerable, fierce—but now, in the quiet of the cabin, she saw something else, something deeper, a weight he carried that went beyond the battles they'd fought, the dangers they'd faced.

"You don't have to keep pretending, you know," she murmured, her voice soft, breaking the silence with a gentle insistence. "Not with me."

He paused, his hands stilling over the logs, his gaze fixed on the fire as though it held some answer he couldn't quite reach. For a moment, he didn't speak, his posture rigid, unyielding, but then he let out a quiet breath, his shoulders relaxing just slightly as he sank down beside her, his gaze fixed on the fire.

"It's not that simple, Rebecca," he said quietly, his voice low, rough, as though the words were dragged from some dark, hidden part of himself. "Pretending's what I do. It's easier that way."

She studied him, her gaze soft, unyielding. "Easier for who?"

He looked at her then, his eyes dark, filled with a mixture of anger and something else, something raw, vulnerable. "For everyone," he muttered, though the words sounded hollow, as though he didn't quite believe them himself.

Rebecca didn't answer, but her hand reached out, her fingers brushing against his in a quiet, gentle reassurance, her touch warm, steady. She didn't push, didn't pry, but her presence was a silent invitation, a reminder that he didn't have to carry it alone, not anymore.

He let out a heavy sigh, his gaze flickering as he looked down at their hands, the warmth of her touch grounding him, steadying him in a way he hadn't expected. "I had a family, once," he said, his voice barely more than a whisper, the words filled with a quiet, aching grief that echoed through the cabin, lingering in the silence.

Rebecca's hand tightened over his, her gaze unwavering as she listened, her expression softened, open, a silent promise that she was there, that she would carry it with him, whatever it was.

He looked away, his gaze fixed on the fire, his jaw clenched, but the words kept coming, unbidden, unstoppable, as though they'd been buried for too long, waiting for this moment. "I lost them," he murmured, his voice rough, edged with a bitterness that cut through the quiet. "My wife, my daughter... they were everything to me. And I failed them."

She felt a pang of sympathy, her heart aching at the quiet, raw pain in his voice, the weight of his confession settling over her like a shroud. She didn't speak, didn't interrupt, but her hand remained steady, a quiet, unwavering support.

Nolan's gaze darkened, his expression hardening as he looked at the fire, his voice laced with a bitterness that seemed to consume him. "I was supposed to protect them. That was my job, my purpose. And I couldn't even do that."

Rebecca's hand tightened over his, her voice soft, filled with a quiet, fierce determination. "You can't blame yourself, Nolan. This world... it's taken so much from all of us. But you don't have to carry it alone."

He looked at her then, his gaze filled with a mixture of anger and something else, something softer, more vulnerable. "You don't understand, Rebecca. I was supposed to be stronger, better. But I failed. And now... now I don't know who I am, or what I'm supposed to be."

She met his gaze, her expression unwavering, her voice steady. "You're still here, aren't you? You're still fighting, still protecting people, still doing everything you can to make this world a little less broken. That counts for something, Nolan."

He let out a bitter laugh, his gaze dropping as he looked down at their hands, the warmth of her touch a quiet, steady reassurance that cut through the darkness, grounding him. "You think so?"

She nodded, her voice soft, filled with a quiet, fierce conviction. "I know so. And whether you want to admit it or not, you're not alone in this anymore."

He looked at her then, his gaze filled with a mixture of gratitude and something else, something unspoken, a quiet, fragile connection that lingered in the silence, a silent acknowledgment of everything they'd been through, everything they'd lost.

Rebecca's hand remained steady, her fingers intertwined with his, her touch warm, grounding, a silent promise that she was there, that she wouldn't leave, no matter how dark the path became. And as the silence settled over them, he felt a quiet, unspoken peace, a sense of belonging that he hadn't felt in years.

They sat together in the quiet of the cabin, the fire crackling softly, the warmth of their shared grief, their shared understanding, settling over them like a fragile, precious shroud. And for the first time, Nolan allowed himself to believe that maybe, just maybe, he didn't have to carry it alone.

Chapter 19: "Team Tensions"

The path to Denver had grown rougher with each mile, the landscape shifting from rocky outcrops to uneven terrain covered in patches of dying grass and brittle shrubs. The air was thick, silent, a grim reminder of the barren world that stretched around them. Rebecca walked beside Nolan, her mind focused on the goal ahead, her thoughts only occasionally drifting to the unspoken tension that had simmered between them since the night in the cabin.

But as they neared the outskirts of what had once been a town, the distant echo of voices caught their attention. They paused, exchanging a wary glance before moving forward, their steps cautious, their senses sharp.

A small group of survivors emerged from the remnants of an old diner, their expressions wary but curious as they took in Rebecca and Nolan's approach. They were a rough-looking bunch, their faces lined with exhaustion, their clothes worn, but there was a faint glimmer of hope in their eyes as they recognized the newcomers.

The group was led by a man who looked to be in his late thirties, tall and muscular, with a sharp, scrutinizing gaze that lingered a little too long on Rebecca. His name, they soon learned, was Alex.

"Well, well," Alex drawled, his gaze sweeping over them with a mixture of amusement and curiosity. "Didn't think I'd be meeting anyone interesting out here, much less someone like you," he said, his eyes resting on Rebecca.

Nolan's expression hardened, his posture shifting as he stepped slightly closer to her, his gaze fixed on Alex with a guarded intensity.

"We're just passing through," he said, his tone cool, dismissive. "Looking for supplies."

Alex raised an eyebrow, a faint smirk playing at his lips as he looked between them, his gaze lingering on Rebecca with a calculated interest that sent a prickle of irritation through her. "Supplies, huh? And here I thought you might be looking for a bit more than that."

Rebecca shot him a look, her tone laced with irony. "Well, that depends. Do you have anything worth taking?"

He chuckled, crossing his arms as he looked at her, his gaze filled with a mixture of admiration and something else, something possessive. "Depends on what you're looking for," he replied, his tone light, though his eyes held a glint of something darker. "You seem capable. Might even be worth sticking around."

Nolan's jaw tightened, his gaze narrowing as he watched the exchange, his stance tense, unyielding. "We don't need any more 'help,'" he said, his tone edged with a warning. "We've managed just fine on our own."

Alex's smirk grew, his gaze shifting to Nolan with a faint glint of amusement, as though he'd recognized a challenge and was more than willing to meet it. "I'm sure you have," he replied, his voice laced with sarcasm. "But maybe she'd be better off with someone who doesn't look like he's been through the grinder."

Rebecca rolled her eyes, stepping between them, her tone dry. "Boys, as much as I enjoy watching you both try to out-brood each other, we have a destination. So let's save the testosterone for something productive."

Alex's gaze softened as he looked at her, though the amusement in his eyes remained. "Feisty. I like that," he said, his voice low, the faintest hint of a challenge there. "Tell me, do you always let him speak for you?"

Rebecca's eyebrow arched, a smirk tugging at her lips. "Only when it's convenient," she replied, shooting a glance at Nolan, her tone filled with wry amusement.

But Nolan wasn't smiling. His gaze remained fixed on Alex, his expression dark, unyielding, a warning glint in his eyes that left little room for negotiation. "We're moving out. Now."

Rebecca felt a flicker of irritation, her pride bristling at his commanding tone, but she held her tongue, her gaze flicking to Alex, who looked more amused than threatened, his smirk deepening as he watched the exchange.

"You know," Alex drawled, his tone light, teasing, "it seems like he's got you on a bit of a leash."

Nolan's fists clenched, his gaze hardening as he took a step forward, his voice low, filled with an edge of warning that left no room for doubt. "Watch it."

Alex chuckled, his gaze taunting, though he didn't back down. "Just making an observation, friend."

Rebecca felt the tension between them escalate, a spark of adrenaline flaring as she stepped between them, her gaze sharp, irritated. "Both of you, enough," she said, her voice steady, commanding, her tone leaving no room for argument. "This isn't the time or place for macho posturing."

Alex's gaze softened, his tone laced with irony as he looked at her. "Apologies, Doc. Didn't mean to ruffle any feathers." But the look he shot at Nolan was filled with unspoken challenge, a glint of satisfaction in his eyes that sent another spark of irritation through her.

Nolan's gaze remained hard, his jaw clenched, but he held his tongue, his expression filled with a quiet, simmering anger that lingered even as they turned to leave, the tension between them palpable.

They'd been walking for hours, the silence between them thick, heavy with the tension that had simmered since the encounter. Rebecca stole a glance at Nolan, his posture tense, his expression hard, his gaze fixed straight ahead, unyielding.

"You know," she said, her tone laced with sarcasm, "you didn't have to get all territorial back there. I'm perfectly capable of handling a little attention."

Nolan shot her a look, his gaze filled with a mixture of irritation and something else, something darker, more possessive. "Attention?" he repeated, his voice edged with sarcasm. "That guy looked at you like you were a prize to be won."

She rolled her eyes, crossing her arms as she looked at him, her tone dry. "And you thought starting a fight was the best way to handle it?"

He didn't answer, his gaze flicking away, though his jaw remained clenched, his expression filled with a frustration that seemed to go beyond the encounter, a simmering tension that lingered between them, unspoken, unresolved.

Rebecca let out a sigh, her voice softening, though the irritation remained. "Look, I appreciate the protective act, but I don't need you to defend my honor every time someone glances my way. I can handle myself."

Nolan's gaze softened, though his expression remained guarded, his voice low, filled with a quiet, restrained frustration. "It's not about you needing protection, Rebecca. It's about respect."

She met his gaze, her expression softening, her voice quiet, though there was a faint, wry amusement in her tone. "Respect or territory?"

He looked away, his expression filled with a mixture of irritation and something else, something unspoken, as though he were struggling to find the right words. "Believe it or not, I'm not interested in starting fights over nothing."

"Could have fooled me," she replied, though her tone was softened by a faint smile, a quiet, unspoken understanding that lingered between them, fragile, precious.

They fell into silence, the tension easing slightly, though the weight of the unspoken lingered, a quiet, fragile connection that neither of them dared to acknowledge fully. But as they walked, Rebecca felt a quiet warmth settle over her, a sense of belonging, of safety, that left her both irritated and comforted, a mixture of pride and exasperation that only seemed to deepen her attachment to him.

And though neither of them spoke, the silence between them was filled with a quiet, unspoken understanding, a connection that grew stronger with each step, binding them together in a way that went beyond words, beyond the tensions that lingered in the air.

But even as they walked, side by side, she knew that this connection, this fragile, precious bond, was something neither of them were ready to face. And for now, that was enough.

Chapter 20: "The Point of No Return"

The world was cloaked in a thick layer of dust, the air dry and stale, with only the faintest hint of sunlight filtering through the haze. Nolan and Rebecca moved quickly through the remnants of the landscape, their steps careful, their senses heightened as they scanned their surroundings. They'd barely had time to process the attack; the hunters had ambushed them in the dead of night, slipping through the shadows like wolves, relentless and ruthless. In the chaos, part of the vaccine had been lost, a blow that left Rebecca visibly shaken, her expression grim, determined.

She stopped suddenly, turning to Nolan with a look of fierce resolve. "I'm going back," she said, her voice steady, though her eyes were filled with a quiet, unyielding determination. "We can't afford to lose any more time. I need new samples. The vaccine is our only chance."

Nolan's gaze hardened, his expression darkening as he took in her words, his stance unyielding. "You're not going back alone."

She shot him a look, a flicker of irritation crossing her face. "I can handle myself, Nolan. This isn't the first time I've taken a risk for the vaccine."

"And it won't be the last," he replied, his tone laced with sarcasm, though his gaze softened slightly as he looked at her, a hint of frustration mingling with something else, something unspoken. "But you don't get to throw yourself into danger without backup."

She crossed her arms, her expression defiant. "I don't remember asking for your permission."

He gave her a look, somewhere between exasperation and amusement. "And yet here we are."

For a moment, they stood in silence, the tension between them thick, charged, as though neither of them was willing to back down. But then she let out a sigh, her posture relaxing just slightly as she looked at him, her gaze filled with a mixture of frustration and something else, something softer, more vulnerable.

"Fine," she muttered, her voice edged with reluctant acceptance. "But if you're coming, you're not pulling rank on me every step of the way."

He raised an eyebrow, his expression filled with a wry amusement. "Pull rank? You know I'm not big on formalities, Doc."

She let out a short, humorless laugh, rolling her eyes. "Could have fooled me."

They moved together, side by side, their steps quiet, purposeful as they navigated the rocky terrain. The silence between them was thick, heavy with unspoken words, a quiet tension that seemed to grow with every step, a reminder of the dangers that loomed around them and the stakes that grew higher with every passing moment.

As they neared the outskirts of an abandoned warehouse, Rebecca paused, her gaze scanning the area, her expression tense, thoughtful. The building was shrouded in shadows, its windows shattered, the walls covered in a thick layer of grime that spoke of years of neglect.

"This is it," she murmured, her voice barely more than a whisper as she turned to Nolan, her expression filled with a mixture of determination and apprehension. "The samples I need are inside."

Nolan nodded, his hand reaching for his weapon, his gaze scanning their surroundings with a calculated precision that left no detail overlooked. "Stay close," he muttered, his tone filled with a quiet, restrained protectiveness that sent a prickle of irritation—and something warmer—through her.

"I thought I wasn't supposed to throw myself into danger," she shot back, though her tone was softened by a faint, reluctant smile.

He huffed, though there was a flicker of amusement in his gaze as he looked at her. "Consider this... preventative care."

They slipped inside, their steps careful, cautious, the silence pressing down on them like a heavy, suffocating shroud. The air was thick, stale, filled with the faint scent of decay, and every shadow seemed to shift and move, a reminder of the dangers that lurked in the darkness.

Rebecca moved quickly, her focus sharp, her gaze fixed on the shelves that lined the walls, each one covered in dust and debris. She found the vials she needed, gathering them with practiced efficiency, her movements swift, precise. But as she turned, her gaze met Nolan's, and for a moment, the urgency faded, replaced by a quiet, unspoken understanding, a connection that lingered in the silence, fragile and precious.

He looked at her, his gaze filled with a mixture of frustration and something softer, more vulnerable, as though he were struggling to find the right words, the right way to convey the weight of everything they'd been through, everything they'd lost.

"Rebecca," he murmured, his voice low, rough, as though the words were dragged from some hidden part of himself. "Why do you keep doing this? Risking everything, pushing yourself to the edge for people you don't even know?"

She met his gaze, her expression softening, her voice quiet, though there was a faint, wry amusement in her tone. "I could ask you the same thing, Captain."

He let out a short, humorless laugh, shaking his head as he looked away, his gaze fixed on the shadows that lined the walls. "Maybe we're both just a little bit crazy."

She took a step closer, her hand reaching out to touch his arm, her fingers brushing against his skin in a quiet, gentle reassurance. "Maybe.

Or maybe we both know that, in a world like this, holding on to something that matters... it's the only way to stay sane."

He looked down at her, his gaze softening, his expression filled with a quiet, unspoken vulnerability that cut through the tension, grounding her, steadying her in a way she hadn't expected. "And what is it that you're holding on to, Doc?"

She hesitated, her gaze dropping as she searched for the right words, the right way to convey the weight of everything she felt, the unspoken bond that had grown between them, a connection that went beyond words, beyond logic.

"I guess... I'm holding on to the hope that there's still something worth saving," she murmured, her voice barely more than a whisper. "That maybe, just maybe, we're not all as lost as we think."

He nodded, his hand reaching up to cover hers, his touch warm, steady, a silent acknowledgment of everything they'd shared, everything they'd endured. "I'd like to believe that, too."

They stood in silence, their hands intertwined, their gazes locked, a quiet, unspoken promise lingering between them, a bond that was as fragile as it was unbreakable. And in that moment, they allowed themselves to let down their guard, to acknowledge the fears, the doubts, the emotions that had simmered beneath the surface, unspoken, unresolved.

But as the silence settled over them, a faint rustle echoed from the shadows, a reminder of the dangers that still lurked, the risks they'd taken. They pulled apart, their gazes sharpening, their focus returning to the mission at hand, though the connection lingered, a quiet, unbreakable bond that neither of them could ignore.

Chapter 21: "Dangerous Allies"

The early morning sun cast a harsh, yellow light across the barren landscape, the cracked earth stretching out in all directions, interrupted only by sparse clusters of broken trees and the occasional rusted wreckage from a world long lost. Nolan and Rebecca moved at a steady pace, the silence between them comfortable, familiar, each of them lost in their own thoughts as they approached the small camp of survivors up ahead.

It had been days since they'd last seen another soul, and even longer since they'd encountered anyone who hadn't tried to kill them. But supplies were running low, and the desperation that clung to the edges of every thought, every decision, had pushed them to take the risk, to seek out allies, if only for the briefest of moments.

As they neared the camp, a man emerged from one of the makeshift tents, his gaze sharp, calculating, his posture relaxed but wary. He was tall, lean, with an unkempt beard and eyes that held a shrewd intelligence, a coldness that sent a prickle of warning down Rebecca's spine. Beside her, she felt Nolan's posture shift, his muscles tensing, a subtle, almost imperceptible adjustment that spoke volumes about his own sense of unease.

"Looks like you two have been through hell," the man said, his voice a smooth, lazy drawl that seemed to mask a deeper, sharper edge. "Looking for some friendly company?"

Nolan shot him a hard look, his expression unyielding. "Friendly isn't exactly the first word that comes to mind."

The man chuckled, his gaze sweeping over them with a faint, amused glint. "Fair enough," he replied, his tone laced with a mocking friendliness. "But out here, beggars can't be choosers. Name's Marcus."

Rebecca exchanged a wary glance with Nolan, her gaze lingering on his face, searching for any hint of recognition or agreement. But his expression remained guarded, his eyes cold, calculating.

"We're just passing through," Rebecca said, her voice calm, steady, though there was a faint edge of suspicion in her tone. "Thought we might trade, if you've got anything useful."

Marcus's smile widened, though there was something dark, something predatory in the way he looked at her, his gaze lingering just a moment too long. "Oh, I think we can work something out," he said, his voice smooth, dripping with a false charm that made her skin crawl.

Nolan stepped forward, his posture shifting, his gaze narrowing as he fixed Marcus with a hard, unyielding stare. "Let's get one thing clear," he said, his voice low, edged with a dangerous calm. "We're here to trade, not to make friends."

Marcus's smile faltered, his gaze flickering with a faint glint of irritation, but he held his ground, his expression darkening as he met Nolan's stare. "Suit yourself," he replied, his tone cool, dismissive. "But out here, a little trust goes a long way."

Nolan didn't answer, but his gaze remained steady, unyielding, his hand resting on his weapon, a silent warning that left little room for interpretation. They moved deeper into the camp, their steps careful, measured, their senses honed to every shift, every flicker of movement that surrounded them.

Rebecca felt the tension between them, the unspoken wariness that lingered in the air, a quiet, simmering threat that seemed to grow with every step, every silent exchange.

As they gathered supplies, Marcus and his crew hovered nearby, watching them with expressions that were far from friendly. Rebecca's instincts prickled with unease, her gaze flicking to Nolan, who returned her look with a subtle nod, a silent acknowledgment that he felt it too—the sense that they were being led into a trap, that danger lurked in every shadow, waiting.

And then, just as they turned to leave, the ambush sprang.

Marcus's crew moved with a practiced precision, their weapons drawn, their faces twisted with a mixture of cruelty and dark amusement as they surrounded them, cutting off every escape route. Rebecca felt her heart pound, her hand reaching instinctively for her weapon, but she knew, even before the fight began, that they were outnumbered, outmatched.

Marcus stepped forward, his expression filled with a smug satisfaction that made her blood boil. "Didn't think you'd get away that easily, did you?"

Nolan's gaze hardened, his hand tightening on his weapon, his voice low, filled with a quiet, deadly calm. "I've gotten out of worse."

Marcus laughed, his gaze flicking between them with a mixture of amusement and disdain. "Oh, I don't doubt it," he replied, his tone mocking, taunting. "But out here, the odds aren't exactly in your favor."

Rebecca exchanged a quick glance with Nolan, her heart pounding, her mind racing as she calculated their options, the risks, the chances of escape. But before she could make a move, Marcus's gaze settled on her, his expression darkening, a cruel smile playing at his lips.

"You know, it's a shame to waste such... potential," he murmured, his gaze lingering on her with a possessive intensity that sent a chill through her. "We could always use someone with your... skills."

Rebecca felt a surge of anger, her voice sharp, defiant. "I'd rather take my chances."

Marcus's smile widened, his expression filled with a dark amusement. "Suit yourself."

But before he could make a move, Nolan was there, his stance shifting, his posture tense, unyielding, his gaze fixed on Marcus with a fierce, unspoken warning that left little room for argument. "Touch her, and I'll make sure it's the last thing you ever do."

Marcus's expression darkened, his gaze flickering with irritation, but he held his ground, his posture shifting as though preparing for a fight. The tension in the air was thick, electric, a quiet, simmering threat that filled every breath, every heartbeat.

But then, in a swift, calculated movement, Nolan lunged, his weapon drawn, his movements precise, deadly. The fight was brutal, chaotic, a blur of motion and sound as they struggled to break free, to escape the trap that had closed around them. Rebecca fought alongside him, her movements swift, instinctive, a fierce determination driving her as they battled their way out, their every move filled with a desperate urgency.

They broke free just as the sun began to sink below the horizon, the camp fading into the distance as they ran, their breaths heavy, their bodies bruised, battered, but alive.

They finally stopped, the silence pressing down on them as they caught their breath, their gazes fixed on the ground, their expressions filled with a mixture of relief and exhaustion. The silence was thick, heavy with the weight of everything they'd just endured, the danger, the betrayal, the fleeting sense of safety that had turned to ashes in an instant.

Rebecca turned to Nolan, her gaze filled with a mixture of frustration and gratitude, though her tone was edged with a faint, weary sarcasm. "So, is this what it takes to make new friends these days?"

Nolan let out a short, humorless laugh, though his expression softened as he looked at her, his gaze filled with a quiet, unspoken protectiveness. "Apparently. But don't get used to it."

She shot him a look, her voice laced with irony. "Oh, believe me, I'm not exactly holding my breath."

They fell into a tense silence, each of them lost in their thoughts, their minds racing with the weight of everything they'd just endured, the dangers they'd faced, the trust that had been shattered. But as they walked, Rebecca felt a quiet, simmering anger, a frustration that gnawed at the edges of her mind, a reminder of the constant, unrelenting dangers that surrounded them.

"How do you do it?" she murmured, her voice barely more than a whisper. "How do you keep going, keep trusting people, when everyone around us is just... waiting to betray you?"

Nolan's gaze flickered, his expression darkening, though there was a faint, wry smile on his lips as he looked at her. "I don't trust people, Rebecca. I trust actions."

She met his gaze, her expression filled with a mixture of curiosity and frustration. "And what about us? What about... this?"

He hesitated, his gaze softening, his voice filled with a quiet, restrained frustration. "I don't know, Doc. But I know that, whatever else happens... I'm not going to let you go down because of someone else's mistakes."

Her gaze softened, her voice barely more than a whisper. "You know, one of these days, your protective streak is going to get you killed."

He looked at her, his expression filled with a mixture of frustration and something softer, something unspoken. "I'm not the one who should be worried," he murmured, his tone laced with irony, though there was a warmth in his gaze that sent a shiver through her. "That virus of yours might spare me, but I'm not sure it's the only thing worth fearing out here."

She gave him a faint smile, though there was a quiet, unspoken tension in her gaze, a mixture of pride and irritation that lingered in the silence, a fragile, precious bond that went beyond words, beyond the dangers that surrounded them.

And as they moved forward, side by side, she felt a quiet, unspoken understanding settle between them, a connection that was as fragile as it was unbreakable. But even as they walked, the shadows closing in around them, she knew that, in a world where allies could turn to enemies in an instant, trust was a luxury they could barely afford.

Chapter 22: "Face to Face with the Past"

The night had settled into a thick, enveloping quiet, broken only by the crackling of the small campfire Nolan had managed to build with the last of their matches and a few pieces of dry wood they'd scavenged along the way. The warmth was a welcome reprieve from the relentless chill that crept in after dark, and the flickering light cast long shadows across the empty, broken landscape around them.

They were miles from the last camp, from the treacherous alliance and the betrayal that had left them running once again. Rebecca could still feel the ache of exhaustion in her bones, the lingering sting of bruises and scratches from their escape. But here, in the solitude of the wilderness, a sense of peace had settled over them, fragile and fleeting, like the soft glow of the fire that separated them.

She watched him from across the flames, her gaze drawn to the lines of his face, the flicker of light and shadow playing across his expression, lending him an air of mystery that only deepened as the silence stretched on between them. He was looking at the fire, his posture relaxed, though there was a tension in his shoulders, a quiet, unspoken weight that she'd come to recognize, to feel in her own chest.

Without fully realizing it, she spoke, her voice soft, breaking the silence that had settled between them. "It wasn't supposed to be like this, you know."

He looked up, his gaze meeting hers, a faint glint of curiosity in his eyes. "What wasn't?"

"This," she murmured, her gaze dropping to the fire, her voice barely more than a whisper. "Any of it. When I started working on the vaccine, it was... it was supposed to save people. To stop the suffering, to give us a chance to start over, to rebuild."

Nolan let out a short, humorless laugh, his gaze flicking back to the flames, his tone edged with irony. "Well, that worked out nicely."

She shot him a look, though there was a faint, rueful smile tugging at her lips. "I know. Believe me, I've spent a lot of sleepless nights wondering where I went wrong."

He looked at her, his gaze softening, his voice quieter, less guarded. "What happened, Rebecca? What made you... decide to do it?"

She hesitated, her gaze dropping to her hands, her fingers tracing patterns in the dirt as she searched for the right words, the right way to tell him without dredging up the pain that still lingered, sharp and unyielding, just beneath the surface.

"I lost my sister," she murmured, her voice barely more than a whisper. "She was... everything to me. My family, my best friend. She got sick, and there was nothing I could do. Nothing anyone could do. I watched her die, helpless, knowing that if I'd just been... faster, better, maybe I could have saved her."

Nolan was silent, his gaze fixed on her, his expression unreadable, though there was a flicker of something in his eyes, a quiet, unspoken sympathy that she hadn't expected. "I'm sorry," he said, his voice low, steady, the sincerity in his tone cutting through the darkness, grounding her.

She let out a shaky breath, a faint, bitter smile playing at her lips. "After she died, I threw myself into my work. The vaccine became... everything. I thought, if I could just find a way to stop it, to save other people... then maybe it wouldn't all be for nothing. Maybe I wouldn't be... so alone."

Nolan looked away, his gaze fixed on the fire, his expression hardening, though his posture softened, a quiet, unspoken vulnerability lingering in his stance. "You're not alone, Rebecca," he murmured, his voice barely more than a whisper, though there was a weight in his words, a sincerity that cut through the silence, settling over them like a fragile, precious shroud.

She looked at him, her gaze softening, her voice quiet, filled with a quiet, aching sincerity. "Neither are you, you know."

He let out a short, humorless laugh, his gaze flicking to her with a faint glint of irony. "Oh, I wouldn't be so sure about that, Doc."

She watched him, studying the lines of his face, the flicker of emotion in his eyes, the faint, guarded expression that he wore like armor. "Nolan," she murmured, her voice barely more than a whisper, a quiet, gentle insistence. "What happened to you?"

He hesitated, his gaze flickering to the fire, his expression hardening as though he were bracing himself, but then he let out a breath, his shoulders relaxing as he looked back at her, a faint, wry smile tugging at his lips.

"I lost my family," he said, his voice low, steady, though there was a bitterness in his tone that cut through the quiet, grounding her. "My wife, my daughter. They were everything to me. And when the world went to hell, I couldn't protect them. Couldn't save them. Just like you."

Rebecca felt a pang of sympathy, her heart aching at the quiet, raw pain in his voice, the weight of his confession settling over her like a shroud. She reached out, her hand brushing against his, a quiet, gentle reassurance, a silent promise that he wasn't alone, that she was there, that she would carry it with him, whatever it was.

Nolan looked down at their hands, his gaze lingering on her touch, the warmth of her fingers grounding him, steadying him in a way he hadn't expected. "You don't have to feel sorry for me, Rebecca," he murmured, his tone laced with irony, though there was a softness in his gaze, a vulnerability that cut through the sarcasm, grounding her. "I've made my peace with it."

She let out a faint, bitter laugh, though there was a warmth in her gaze, a quiet, unspoken understanding. "I don't feel sorry for you, Nolan. I just... I understand."

They fell into silence, the weight of their shared losses, their shared grief settling over them like a fragile, unbreakable bond. The fire crackled softly, its warm glow casting long shadows across their faces, illuminating the lines of their expressions, the quiet, unspoken connection that lingered between them, a bond that went beyond words, beyond pain.

Rebecca looked at him, her gaze lingering on the lines of his face, the flicker of light in his eyes, the faint, guarded expression that hid so much more than he was willing to show. And in that moment, she felt a quiet, unspoken love, a deep, aching connection that left her breathless, filled her with a sense of belonging, of understanding that she hadn't felt in years.

But before she could speak, before she could find the words to express the weight of everything she felt, he looked at her, a faint, wry smile tugging at his lips, his voice filled with a quiet, mocking humor that cut through the tension, grounding her, steadying her.

"You might want to look at the fire, Doc," he murmured, his tone laced with irony, though there was a warmth in his gaze that belied his words. "Wouldn't want you to get burned."

She let out a soft laugh, though her gaze remained fixed on him, her voice filled with a quiet, aching sincerity. "Maybe I'm willing to take that risk."

He looked at her, his gaze softening, his expression filled with a quiet, unspoken understanding, a connection that went beyond words, beyond pain, a bond that was as fragile as it was unbreakable. And in that moment, they allowed themselves to let down their guard, to acknowledge the fears, the doubts, the emotions that had simmered beneath the surface, unspoken, unresolved.

But as the silence settled over them, as the fire crackled softly in the night, they both knew that there were some things that couldn't be said, some emotions that couldn't be fully expressed. And for now, that was enough.

Chapter 23: "Maze of Dangers"

The entrance to the old subway tunnel loomed before them, a gaping maw that stretched into darkness, the faint smell of decay and dampness seeping from its depths. Rebecca felt a shiver run down her spine as she peered into the shadows, the faint echo of water dripping somewhere in the distance creating a hollow, unsettling sound that seemed to reverberate through the cold, stale air.

Beside her, Nolan adjusted his gear, his gaze fixed on the darkness with a mixture of wariness and grim determination. His hand rested on his weapon, his posture tense, ready for anything that might lurk within the shadows.

"Let me guess," he murmured, his tone laced with sarcasm as he glanced at her. "You're going to tell me you have a deep-seated fear of tunnels now?"

Rebecca shot him a look, her expression unimpressed. "Funny. I'd say being forced to walk into a literal pit of despair filled with god-knows-what isn't exactly a walk in the park."

He smirked, though his gaze remained fixed on the darkness, his voice a low, mocking drawl. "Trust me, Doc. I've seen worse."

She rolled her eyes, though there was a faint, reluctant smile tugging at her lips. "Of course you have."

They moved forward, the darkness swallowing them as they entered the tunnel, the faint light from above fading until it was nothing more than a distant memory. Nolan switched on his flashlight, the beam cutting through the gloom, illuminating the walls lined with faded posters and graffiti, relics from a world long gone.

The silence was thick, oppressive, pressing down on them like a weight as they made their way deeper into the tunnel. Each step echoed, the sound amplified in the narrow space, and every flicker of movement, every distant creak seemed to reverberate, filling the air with an unspoken tension that only grew heavier with every passing moment.

As they moved, the faint sound of shuffling footsteps reached them, a reminder of the dangers that lurked within these dark, narrow corridors. The infected, mindless and relentless, drawn to any sign of life, any sound, any movement.

Rebecca's hand tightened on her weapon, her heart pounding as she glanced at Nolan, her voice barely more than a whisper. "How many do you think are down here?"

He shrugged, his gaze scanning the darkness, his expression calm, unbothered, though there was a faint, wary glint in his eyes. "Enough to make this a bad idea."

She shot him a look, her tone dry. "Comforting."

They pressed on, their steps careful, measured, their senses honed to every flicker of movement, every shift in the shadows. The air was thick, damp, filled with the faint, musty scent of decay, and every now and then, the beam of Nolan's flashlight would catch a glimpse of something pale and still, a reminder of those who hadn't been so lucky.

As they rounded a corner, the sound of voices echoed from further down the tunnel, sharp, guttural, the unmistakable tone of hunters, their laughter and jeers carrying through the silence. Rebecca felt a chill run down her spine, her gaze flicking to Nolan, whose posture had stiffened, his gaze narrowing.

"Great," he muttered, his voice laced with sarcasm. "As if the infected weren't enough."

Rebecca felt her heart race, her mind calculating their options, the risks, the chances of escape. But before she could speak, Nolan grabbed her arm, pulling her into a narrow alcove, the walls pressing close around them as they crouched in the shadows, their bodies pressed together in the tight, confined space.

She froze, her pulse quickening as she felt the warmth of his body against hers, the steady, grounding presence that seemed to fill every inch of the narrow alcove. His arm brushed against her shoulder, his hand resting just inches from hers, and for a moment, she was acutely aware of every detail, every breath, every heartbeat that echoed in the silence.

The voices grew louder, the sound of footsteps drawing closer, filling the air with a sense of impending danger, a reminder of the deadly game they were playing. She held her breath, her gaze fixed on the shadows, her mind racing as she calculated the odds, the risks, the consequences of every move.

But then she felt it—his hand, brushing against hers, a light, fleeting touch that sent a thrill through her, a quiet, unspoken connection that lingered in the silence, a bond that went beyond words, beyond logic. She felt a surge of warmth, a flicker of something deeper, more intense, and before she could stop herself, she glanced up at him, meeting his gaze in the dim light.

Nolan looked down at her, his expression unreadable, his gaze filled with a mixture of frustration and something else, something darker, more intense, a flicker of emotion that he quickly masked with a faint, wry smirk.

"Don't get any ideas, Doc," he murmured, his voice barely more than a whisper, though there was a warmth in his tone that belied his words. "This isn't exactly my idea of a romantic evening."

She let out a faint, shaky laugh, though her gaze remained fixed on his, her voice filled with a quiet, defiant humor. "Oh, don't worry. The feeling's mutual."

They fell into silence, the tension between them thick, electric, a quiet, unspoken connection that lingered in the narrow space, a bond that was as fragile as it was unbreakable. And for a moment, they allowed themselves to forget the dangers that lurked around them, the infected, the hunters, the unyielding darkness that threatened to consume them.

But as the voices grew louder, closer, a reminder of the imminent danger that surrounded them, they pulled back, their gazes sharpening, their focus returning to the task at hand. Nolan shifted, his posture tensing as he glanced around the corner, his expression hardening as he took in the figures moving through the tunnel, their movements swift, predatory.

He turned back to her, his gaze steady, his voice low, edged with a quiet, restrained protectiveness. "Stay close, and follow my lead."

She nodded, her gaze steady, though her heart raced with a mixture of fear and adrenaline, a reminder of the dangers that surrounded them, the risks they'd taken, the stakes that grew higher with every passing moment.

They moved through the shadows, their steps careful, precise, each movement calculated, deliberate, a delicate dance of survival. The hunters moved ahead, oblivious to their presence, their laughter and jeers filling the air, a dark, ominous reminder of the cruelty that lurked in the depths of this broken world.

Rebecca felt her heart pound, her mind racing as they slipped through the darkness, her every sense honed to the flicker of shadows, the distant echo of footsteps, the faint, hollow breaths of the infected that lurked in the corners, waiting, watching.

As they rounded a corner, the path ahead split into two, each tunnel stretching into darkness, the faint, distant echo of footsteps and shuffling breaths filling the silence. Nolan paused, his gaze flicking between the paths, his expression hard, calculating.

"Left or right?" she whispered, her voice barely more than a breath.

He shot her a look, his tone laced with sarcasm. "Oh, sure, let's make it a fifty-fifty gamble. Why not?"

She rolled her eyes, though her gaze softened, a faint, reluctant smile tugging at her lips. "Got any better ideas, Captain?"

He huffed, though there was a flicker of amusement in his gaze as he looked at her, his expression softening, a quiet, unspoken connection lingering between them. "Fine. Left it is."

They moved down the left path, their steps quick, silent, their senses honed to every shift in the darkness, every flicker of movement that seemed to close in around them. The air grew thicker, colder, the smell of decay filling the narrow space, a reminder of the dangers that lurked just beyond the edge of their vision.

And then, without warning, a figure lunged from the shadows, its hollow eyes fixed on them, its mouth open in a silent, endless scream. Rebecca's heart leapt, her body tensing as she drew her weapon, her movements swift, instinctive, a fierce determination driving her as she fought back, her every move filled with a desperate urgency.

Nolan was beside her, his movements precise, calculated, each strike a reminder of his skill, his strength, the unyielding protectiveness that lingered beneath his sarcasm, his irony. They fought side by side, their every move in sync, a delicate, deadly dance of survival that left no room for hesitation, no time for doubt.

When the last infected fell, they stood in silence, their breaths heavy, their gazes fixed on each other, a quiet, unspoken understanding passing between them, a bond that went beyond words, beyond fear, a connection that was as fragile as it was unbreakable.

Rebecca looked at him, her gaze filled with a mixture of gratitude and something else, something deeper, more intense, a quiet, unspoken attachment that left her breathless, filled her with a sense of belonging, of understanding that she hadn't felt in years.

But before she could speak, before she could find the words to express the weight of everything she felt, he looked at her, a faint, wry smile tugging at his lips, his voice filled with a quiet, mocking humor that cut through the tension, grounding her, steadying her.

"Still think this was a good idea, Doc?" he murmured, his tone laced with irony, though there was a warmth in his gaze that belied his words.

She let out a soft laugh, though her gaze remained fixed on him, her voice filled with a quiet, aching sincerity. "Let's just say I'm glad I didn't have to face it alone."

He looked at her, his gaze softening, his expression filled with a quiet, unspoken understanding, a connection that went beyond words, beyond pain, a bond that was as fragile as it was unbreakable. And in that moment, they allowed themselves to let down their guard, to acknowledge the fears, the doubts, the emotions that had simmered beneath the surface, unspoken, unresolved.

But as the silence settled over them, as the darkness closed in around them once more, they both knew that there were some things that couldn't be said, some emotions that couldn't be fully expressed. And for now, that was enough.

Chapter 24: "Through Ice and Fire"

The biting cold hit them like a wall as they emerged from the darkness of the tunnels, stepping into a harsh, frozen landscape that stretched out before them in stark, unforgiving silence. Snow blanketed the ground, covering the jagged rocks and sparse trees in a layer of white that gleamed under the weak light filtering through the dense clouds above. The wind howled through the mountains, carrying with it a chill that seemed to cut straight to the bone, leaving a sharp, stinging ache in its wake.

Rebecca wrapped her arms around herself, her teeth chattering as she looked out at the endless expanse of white, her breath visible in small, wispy clouds that dissipated into the cold air. "Great," she muttered, her voice muffled by the scarf she'd pulled over her mouth. "Just what I needed—an impromptu adventure through the Arctic."

Beside her, Nolan adjusted his pack, his expression grim as he scanned the horizon, his posture tense, his hand resting on the hilt of his weapon, though there was little threat beyond the unforgiving weather. "Could be worse," he replied, his tone dry, though there was a faint smirk tugging at the corners of his lips. "At least it's not raining."

Rebecca shot him a look, her expression somewhere between exasperation and reluctant amusement. "Oh, how comforting," she replied, her voice dripping with sarcasm. "I'll make sure to be grateful as I freeze to death."

Nolan's smirk widened, though his gaze softened slightly as he looked at her, his expression filled with a quiet, unspoken concern that he quickly masked with a faint shrug. "Well, look on the bright side," he murmured, his tone laced with irony. "At least we're out of those tunnels."

She let out a short, humorless laugh, though there was a faint glimmer of warmth in her gaze. "Yes, because being buried under a mountain of snow is such a refreshing change of pace."

He huffed, his gaze flicking to the sky, his expression hardening as he took in the thick clouds rolling in, the wind picking up speed, carrying with it a chill that seemed to cut through even the thickest layers of clothing. "Looks like a storm's coming in," he muttered, his voice filled with a quiet, restrained frustration.

Rebecca let out a sigh, her voice soft, filled with a mixture of resignation and irritation. "Of course it is."

They moved forward, their steps slow, cautious, each step a battle against the biting wind, the thick snow that clung to their boots, sapping their strength with every step. The silence was thick, heavy, pressing down on them like a weight, broken only by the howling wind and the crunch of snow beneath their feet.

As they climbed higher into the mountains, the storm grew stronger, the wind picking up speed, carrying with it a freezing mist that clung to their clothes, their skin, leaving a thin layer of ice in its wake. Rebecca felt her strength waning, her movements growing sluggish, her fingers numb, her body shivering despite her best efforts to keep moving.

Nolan noticed, his gaze sharpening as he looked at her, his expression filled with a mixture of concern and irritation. "We need to stop," he said, his voice firm, leaving little room for argument.

Rebecca shot him a look, her voice sharp, though there was a faint tremor in her tone. "Keep moving. I'm fine."

He raised an eyebrow, his expression unimpressed. "Sure you are," he replied, his tone laced with sarcasm. "That's why you look like you're about to keel over any second now."

She let out a frustrated sigh, though there was a faint, grudging acceptance in her gaze as she met his eyes. "Fine. But just for a few minutes."

They found a small, sheltered alcove between the rocks, a narrow space that offered little in the way of warmth but shielded them from the worst of the wind. Nolan dropped his pack, pulling out a thin, insulated blanket and spreading it out on the ground, his movements swift, efficient.

Rebecca sank down beside him, wrapping her arms around herself as she tried to suppress the shivers that wracked her body, her teeth chattering as she looked at him, her gaze filled with a mixture of gratitude and irritation. "You know, this whole 'macho protector' act is starting to wear thin."

He shot her a look, his tone laced with irony. "Just trying to keep you alive, Doc. But by all means, feel free to freeze if it makes you feel more independent."

She let out a faint laugh, though her gaze softened, a quiet, unspoken warmth lingering in her expression as she looked at him. "Touché."

They sat in silence, the cold pressing down on them, filling the air with a heavy, suffocating chill that seemed to seep into their bones, leaving them both shivering, their breaths visible in small clouds that hung in the air before dissipating into the darkness.

Nolan shifted, his gaze flicking to her, his expression hardening as he took in her pale face, her trembling hands. Without a word, he pulled her closer, wrapping the blanket around them both, his arm slipping around her shoulders as he held her against him, his body warm, steady, grounding her, filling her with a sense of safety she hadn't realized she needed.

She froze, her pulse quickening as she felt the warmth of his body against hers, the steady, reassuring presence that seemed to fill every inch of the narrow space. Her hands were pressed against his chest, her face resting just inches from his, and for a moment, she was acutely aware of every detail, every heartbeat, every breath that echoed in the silence.

"This doesn't mean I like you, you know," she muttered, her voice barely more than a whisper, though there was a faint, teasing glint in her eyes.

Nolan huffed, a faint smile tugging at the corners of his lips. "The feeling's mutual, Doc," he replied, his tone laced with sarcasm, though there was a warmth in his gaze that belied his words. "Let's just call it... survival."

She let out a soft laugh, her gaze lingering on his face, the lines of his expression, the flicker of emotion in his eyes, a quiet, unspoken connection that went beyond words, beyond logic. Her fingers tightened against his chest, her gaze softening as she met his eyes, the warmth of his body grounding her, filling her with a sense of belonging that left her breathless.

For a moment, they were both silent, their gazes locked, a quiet, unspoken bond settling between them, fragile and precious. She felt his arms tighten around her, his hand resting against her back, his touch warm, steady, a silent promise that he wouldn't let go, that he wouldn't leave her, not now, not ever.

"Can't say you're the easiest company," he murmured, his voice barely more than a whisper, though there was a faint, teasing warmth in his tone.

She raised an eyebrow, a faint smirk tugging at her lips. "Right back at you, Captain."

They fell into silence, the warmth of their shared presence, their shared connection filling the air with a quiet, unspoken understanding. The storm raged around them, the wind howling through the mountains, but in that moment, it was as though they were the only two people in the world, bound together by a fragile, unbreakable bond.

Rebecca let out a shaky breath, her voice barely more than a whisper, though there was a faint, aching sincerity in her tone. "Nolan... I don't know what's going to happen. I don't know if we're even going to make it to Denver. But... I'm glad I'm here. With you."

He looked down at her, his expression softening, his voice filled with a quiet, unspoken vulnerability that left her breathless. "Yeah. Me too."

For a moment, they held each other's gaze, a quiet, unspoken connection passing between them, a bond that went beyond words, beyond the dangers that surrounded them. And as the storm raged around them, as the cold pressed down on them, they both knew that whatever happened, whatever dangers they faced, they would face it together, bound by a connection that was as fragile as it was unbreakable.

Chapter 25: "When It All Falls Apart"

They spotted the settlement just as the sky began to lighten, the faint glow of dawn breaking through the dense layer of clouds that had hung over them for days. It was a small outpost, tucked into the shadow of the mountains, the remnants of what must have once been a remote logging town. A scattering of tents and makeshift shelters filled the space between the buildings, and even from a distance, Rebecca could see the weary, cautious faces of those who lingered near the entrance, their eyes tracking her and Nolan's approach.

Nolan slowed his pace, his gaze narrowing as he took in the settlement, his posture tense, alert. "Looks cozy," he muttered, his tone laced with sarcasm. "A place where dreams go to die."

Rebecca shot him a look, though a faint, hopeful smile played at her lips. "At this point, I'd settle for any place where I don't have to sleep with one eye open."

He huffed, a faint smirk tugging at the corners of his mouth. "Good luck with that."

They approached the entrance, their movements slow, cautious, their senses honed to every flicker of movement, every shadow that lingered in the corners of the settlement. A guard stepped forward, his posture wary, though there was a faint, reluctant warmth in his gaze as he took in their battered, exhausted appearances.

"Passing through?" he asked, his voice gruff, though there was a note of curiosity, a faint glimmer of recognition as he glanced at the weapon slung over Nolan's shoulder, the determined set of Rebecca's jaw.

Nolan exchanged a glance with Rebecca, his gaze flicking back to the guard, his expression unyielding. "Looking for somewhere safe to rest," he replied, his tone calm, though there was a faint edge of warning, a quiet, restrained protectiveness in his stance.

The guard nodded, stepping aside with a faint gesture. "Welcome to what's left of civilization," he muttered, his voice laced with irony. "If you can call it that."

They moved inside, weaving through the narrow pathways that wound between the makeshift shelters, the remnants of hope and desperation lingering in the air like a heavy, suffocating shroud. The people here were survivors, hardened by the unforgiving world they inhabited, but there was a quiet resilience in their gazes, a flicker of determination that filled Rebecca with a faint, cautious hope.

They found a small, sheltered corner near the edge of the settlement, a patch of ground protected from the wind, offering a brief reprieve from the relentless cold. Rebecca sank down, letting out a weary sigh as she leaned back against the wall, her gaze drifting over the people around them, the quiet, unspoken sense of camaraderie that filled the air, a reminder of the fragile bonds that held them all together.

For the first time in days, she felt a flicker of relief, a faint, fragile sense of hope that maybe, just maybe, they'd found a place where they could catch their breath, regroup, and plan their next move.

But the reprieve was short-lived.

The attack came without warning, a sudden, violent explosion that ripped through the air, sending debris flying, the screams and shouts of the survivors filling the settlement as they scrambled to find cover, their movements frantic, desperate.

Nolan grabbed Rebecca's arm, pulling her to her feet, his voice a low, urgent murmur. "Move. Now."

They stumbled through the chaos, their steps quick, unsteady, their gazes flicking to the shadows, the flicker of movement that lurked in the corners, a reminder of the dangers that surrounded them. The attackers moved through the settlement with a ruthless efficiency, their faces hidden, their intentions clear as they struck with a brutal, unyielding precision.

Rebecca clutched the bag that held the vaccine samples, her heart pounding as she calculated their options, the risks, the chances of escape. But in the chaos, a figure lunged at her, grabbing the bag and wrenching it from her grasp, the samples slipping from her fingers, tumbling to the ground in a scattered mess of broken glass and shattered vials.

"No!" Her voice was a strangled cry, filled with desperation, a raw, aching grief that cut through the noise, grounding her, anchoring her in the middle of the chaos. She dropped to her knees, her hands scrambling over the broken shards, the remnants of her work, her mission, her purpose, scattered at her feet, lost in an instant.

Nolan was there in an instant, pulling her to her feet, his grip firm, steady, a quiet, unyielding strength that cut through her despair. "Rebecca, we have to go. Now."

She looked up at him, her gaze filled with a mixture of horror and grief, her voice barely more than a whisper. "It's gone, Nolan. Everything... it's all gone."

He tightened his grip on her arm, his voice a low, fierce murmur, filled with a quiet, restrained frustration. "Then we'll get it back."

She shook her head, her voice trembling, filled with a quiet, aching despair. "You don't understand. Those samples... they were our last chance. Our only chance."

He met her gaze, his expression hard, determined, his voice filled with a quiet, unspoken promise. "Then we'll make a new one."

Before she could respond, he pulled her away, leading her through the chaos, his movements swift, precise, his focus sharp, unyielding. They moved through the settlement, weaving between the scattered remnants of what had once been a fragile, hopeful community, the sounds of destruction filling the air, a reminder of the relentless, unforgiving world that surrounded them.

When they finally reached the edge of the settlement, the fires casting a harsh, orange glow over the wreckage, Rebecca stopped, her gaze fixed on the distant, dark outline of the mountains, the path that stretched before them, filled with dangers, risks, uncertainties.

She turned to him, her voice barely more than a whisper, though there was a faint, desperate hope in her tone. "You really think we can get it back?"

He looked at her, his expression softened, his voice filled with a quiet, unspoken sincerity that left her breathless. "I wouldn't have dragged you out of there if I didn't."

She let out a shaky breath, her gaze softening as she looked at him, her voice filled with a quiet, aching gratitude. "Thank you."

He shrugged, though there was a faint, reluctant warmth in his gaze, a quiet, unspoken attachment that he quickly masked with a faint smirk. "Don't thank me yet. We haven't even started."

She gave him a faint smile, though her expression was filled with a quiet, determined resolve, a reminder of the purpose that had driven her, the mission that had kept her going, even in the face of overwhelming odds.

But before she could speak, he looked at her, his expression hardening, his voice filled with a quiet, restrained protectiveness. "We're getting that vaccine back, Rebecca. Together."

Her gaze softened, her heart aching with a mixture of relief and something deeper, more intense, a quiet, unspoken bond that lingered between them, a connection that went beyond words, beyond pain, beyond the unrelenting chaos that surrounded them.

And in that moment, as they stood on the edge of the ruined settlement, the fires casting long shadows over the mountains, she knew that whatever happened, whatever dangers they faced, they would face it together, bound by a bond that was as fragile as it was unbreakable.

Chapter 26: "The Rescue Plan"

The night was pitch-dark, the sky cloaked in thick, heavy clouds that blocked out even the faintest glimmer of moonlight, casting the mountains and the ruined settlement into a deep, oppressive darkness. The cold bit into them, sharp and relentless, but neither Rebecca nor Nolan seemed to notice as they crouched over a makeshift map drawn in the dirt, their faces illuminated only by the faint glow of a small, dying fire.

Nolan held a stick in his hand, tracing a path through the uneven lines he'd scratched into the ground, his gaze focused, his expression hard, unyielding. His plan was simple, direct, and just this side of suicidal, but it was the best they could come up with given the limited time and resources.

Rebecca watched him, her gaze flicking between his face and the map, a faint, uneasy knot forming in her stomach as she took in the details of his plan, the risks, the slim chances of success. "So, you're just going to stroll into Lucifer's camp, grab the vaccine, and stroll back out?" she murmured, her tone laced with sarcasm, though there was a faint edge of worry in her voice.

He shot her a look, his expression filled with a mixture of dry amusement and grim determination. "Something like that," he replied, his tone calm, though there was a glint of humor in his eyes. "Unless you've got a better idea."

She let out a short, humorless laugh, though her gaze softened slightly as she looked at him, her voice barely more than a whisper. "Just one. Don't get yourself killed."

He huffed, a faint smirk tugging at the corners of his mouth. "What, and deprive you of my endless wisdom and life-changing advice?"

She rolled her eyes, though there was a faint, reluctant smile playing at her lips. "Oh, please. I think I'd survive."

They fell into silence, the tension between them thick, heavy, a quiet, unspoken acknowledgment of the risks, the dangers that lay ahead. She knew, deep down, that his plan was the only way, that they had no other choice, but the thought of him facing Lucifer and his hunters alone, with only a vague map and a slim chance of success, filled her with a quiet, gnawing fear she couldn't quite shake.

As he finished outlining the route he planned to take, he glanced up at her, his gaze steady, his expression softened by a quiet, unspoken sincerity. "Listen, Rebecca," he murmured, his voice low, steady, though there was a faint edge of humor in his tone, an attempt to mask the weight of what he was about to say. "I know it's a long shot. But I've gotten out of worse."

She looked at him, her expression softened by a quiet, aching gratitude, a silent acknowledgment of everything he was willing to risk, everything he was willing to do to keep her mission, her purpose alive. "Thank you," she murmured, her voice barely more than a whisper, though there was a warmth in her gaze, a quiet, unspoken attachment that lingered in the silence between them.

He shrugged, his gaze dropping back to the map, though there was a faint, reluctant warmth in his expression, a quiet, unspoken connection that he quickly masked with a faint smirk. "Don't get all sentimental on me, Doc," he muttered, his tone laced with sarcasm. "I'm just in it for the adrenaline rush."

She let out a soft laugh, though her gaze remained fixed on him, her voice filled with a quiet, aching sincerity. "Just... be careful, okay?"

He looked up at her, his gaze steady, his expression softened by a quiet, unspoken understanding, a bond that went beyond words, beyond logic, a connection that was as fragile as it was unbreakable. "I'll do my best," he murmured, his voice low, filled with a quiet, restrained protectiveness that left her breathless.

They fell into silence again, the weight of everything they'd endured, everything they'd lost, settling over them like a heavy, suffocating shroud. She reached out, her hand resting on his, her touch warm, grounding, a silent promise that she would be there, waiting, that she wouldn't let him face it alone.

He looked down at her hand, his gaze lingering on her fingers, the warmth of her touch a quiet, steady reassurance that filled him with a sense of belonging he hadn't felt in years, a connection that went beyond pain, beyond fear. He let out a short, humorless laugh, though there was a faint, reluctant warmth in his tone. "I'll be back," he muttered, his voice filled with a quiet, mocking humor. "Wouldn't want you to go soft without me around to keep you in line."

She smiled, her gaze softened by a quiet, unspoken attachment, though her voice was laced with a faint, teasing sarcasm. "Oh, I'm sure I'd manage."

They held each other's gaze for a long moment, a quiet, unspoken connection passing between them, a bond that went beyond words, beyond logic, a connection that was as fragile as it was unbreakable. And in that moment, as they stood on the edge of the firelight, with only the darkness stretching out before them, they both knew that whatever happened, whatever dangers they faced, they would face it together, bound by a bond that was as fragile as it was unbreakable.

Without another word, he turned, disappearing into the darkness, his steps silent, measured, his figure swallowed by the shadows, leaving her standing alone, her gaze fixed on the path he'd taken, a quiet, unspoken promise lingering in the air between them, a bond that went beyond words, beyond pain, beyond the unrelenting chaos that surrounded them.

Chapter 27: "Broken Chains"

The air inside Lucifer's camp was thick with the stench of damp earth, sweat, and something darker, something acrid that filled the back of the throat, coating it in a bitter, metallic taste that made it hard to breathe. They moved in silence, their steps careful, measured, each movement calculated to avoid detection, their senses honed to every flicker of shadow, every distant echo of footsteps.

Nolan led the way, his posture tense, his gaze sharp, a fierce concentration etched into every line of his face as he navigated the narrow corridors of the compound, the dim light casting long shadows over the walls, lending the place an eerie, almost nightmarish quality. Behind him, Rebecca moved quietly, her footsteps light, her gaze fixed on the path ahead, her body tensed with a mixture of fear and determination.

The plan had been simple: get in, locate the vaccine, and get out before anyone noticed they were there. But as they rounded a corner, slipping into a darkened hallway that stretched out before them like a tunnel into oblivion, they heard it—a faint, muffled cry, a sound that cut through the silence like a knife, sharp and piercing, filled with a desperation that sent a shiver down Rebecca's spine.

She stopped, her gaze flicking to the door on their left, the sound coming from behind it, a low, guttural murmur that seemed to resonate through the walls, filling the air with a sense of dread, of unspoken horror. She glanced at Nolan, her eyes wide, filled with a quiet, unspoken plea, a silent question that lingered in the air between them, heavy with unspoken tension.

He shot her a look, his expression hard, unyielding, his voice barely more than a whisper. "Keep moving, Rebecca. We're here for the vaccine, remember?"

She hesitated, her gaze lingering on the door, her expression filled with a mixture of fear and compassion, a quiet, aching determination that cut through her hesitation, grounding her, steadying her. "I can't just leave them, Nolan. They're prisoners—people, just like us."

He let out a low, frustrated sigh, though there was a faint, reluctant warmth in his gaze as he looked at her, his voice filled with a quiet, restrained protectiveness. "And if we try to free them, we're as good as dead."

She met his gaze, her expression unwavering, her voice filled with a quiet, fierce conviction. "Maybe. But if we leave them here, then what are we fighting for? What's the point of any of this?"

He looked away, his jaw clenched, his expression hardening as he weighed their options, calculating the risks, the chances of success, the possibility of escape. He knew, deep down, that she was right, that leaving these people behind would be a betrayal of everything they stood for, everything they'd fought to protect.

"Fine," he muttered, his tone laced with sarcasm, though there was a faint, reluctant warmth in his gaze, a quiet, unspoken acknowledgment of her strength, her compassion, her fierce, unyielding determination. "But if we die doing this, you're explaining it to whatever afterlife we end up in."

She shot him a faint smile, her voice filled with a quiet, wry humor. "Deal."

They moved toward the door, their steps quick, cautious, their senses honed to every flicker of movement, every shift in the shadows. Nolan reached for the handle, his grip firm, his posture tense, his gaze fixed on the door as he prepared to face whatever waited on the other side.

The room beyond was dimly lit, filled with the faint, sickly glow of a single, flickering bulb that cast long shadows over the walls, lending the space an eerie, almost surreal quality. The prisoners were huddled together in the corner, their faces pale, gaunt, filled with a quiet, unspoken desperation that cut through the silence, filling the air with a sense of suffocating despair.

Rebecca felt a pang of sympathy, her heart aching at the sight of their hollow eyes, their broken expressions, a reminder of the horrors they'd endured, the darkness they'd been forced to face. She moved toward them, her gaze filled with a quiet, unspoken compassion, her voice soft, soothing, a gentle reassurance that cut through the tension, grounding them, steadying them.

"It's okay," she murmured, her voice barely more than a whisper, though there was a fierce determination in her tone, a quiet, unyielding promise that she wouldn't let them face this alone. "We're here to get you out."

One of the prisoners looked up, his eyes filled with a mixture of fear and disbelief, his voice trembling, barely more than a breath. "You... you're here to help us?"

She nodded, her gaze steady, filled with a quiet, unspoken strength that cut through the despair, filling the air with a sense of hope, a fragile, precious light in the midst of the darkness. "Yes," she murmured, her voice filled with a fierce, unwavering conviction. "We're not leaving without you."

Nolan moved to the door, his gaze flicking to the hallway, his posture tense, alert, his senses honed to every flicker of movement, every distant echo of footsteps. "We don't have much time," he muttered, his tone filled with a quiet, restrained frustration. "Let's get this done before someone notices we're here."

Rebecca moved quickly, her hands steady as she helped the prisoners to their feet, her voice filled with a quiet, soothing reassurance, a gentle reminder that they were no longer alone, that they didn't have to face this darkness on their own.

As they made their way back toward the exit, Rebecca noticed the faint, reluctant admiration in Nolan's gaze, a quiet, unspoken acknowledgment of her strength, her compassion, her fierce, unyielding determination. And in that moment, as he looked at her, a faint, reluctant smile tugged at the corners of his mouth, a quiet, unspoken warmth that cut through the tension, grounding them, steadying them.

"You know," he murmured, his voice barely more than a whisper, though there was a faint, ironic warmth in his tone, a quiet, mocking humor that belied his words. "I never thought I'd say this, but... I actually admire that ridiculous, self-sacrificing streak of yours."

She shot him a look, her gaze softened by a quiet, unspoken attachment, though there was a faint, teasing smile tugging at her lips. "Who knew you were capable of admiration?"

He let out a short, humorless laugh, though there was a faint, reluctant warmth in his gaze, a quiet, unspoken connection that lingered in the silence between them, a bond that went beyond words, beyond pain, beyond the dangers that surrounded them. "Don't get used to it, Doc."

They fell into silence, the weight of everything they'd endured, everything they'd lost, settling over them like a heavy, suffocating shroud. But in that moment, as they moved through the shadows, the faint, flickering light casting long shadows over their faces, they both knew that whatever happened, whatever dangers they faced, they would face it together, bound by a connection that was as fragile as it was unbreakable.

Chapter 28: "Ghosts and Reality"

The air was thick with tension as they navigated through the narrow corridors of the camp, each step heavy, deliberate, the distant echoes of footsteps a reminder that their time was running out. The freed hostages moved in tense silence behind them, their faces pale, eyes darting to every shadow, every flicker of movement, their fear a palpable weight that filled the space, pressing down on them like a suffocating shroud.

Nolan moved with a fierce, unyielding determination, his gaze sharp, focused, his posture tense, every line of his body honed to the task of getting them out alive. But even as he led the group, a cold dread coiled in his gut, a nagging sense that something wasn't right, that their escape wouldn't be as simple as slipping back into the shadows.

They rounded a corner, the dim light casting long shadows over the walls, and then he saw him—standing at the end of the hallway, arms crossed, a faint, mocking smile playing at the corners of his mouth.

Lucifer.

The sight of him was like a punch to the gut, a brutal reminder of everything he'd tried to bury, everything he'd tried to forget. The man before him was older now, his face lined with the marks of a life filled with cruelty and ambition, but there was no mistaking the cold, calculating glint in his eyes, the sharp, predatory smile that cut through the darkness like a blade.

For a moment, Nolan was frozen, his mind flooded with memories, flashes of a past he'd spent years trying to escape. And then, as if sensing his shock, Lucifer's smile widened, his gaze fixed on Nolan with a mixture of amusement and something darker, something twisted, a reminder of the shared history that lingered between them like a ghost.

"Nolan," he murmured, his voice smooth, mocking, filled with a quiet, deadly amusement. "It's been a long time."

Nolan clenched his fists, his jaw tightening as he forced himself to hold Lucifer's gaze, his mind racing, a storm of anger, fear, and something else—something raw and unyielding—swirling within him.

"Not long enough," he replied, his voice low, edged with a quiet, restrained fury that cut through the silence, grounding him, steadying him.

Lucifer chuckled, a dark, hollow sound that echoed through the hallway, filling the air with a sense of unease, a reminder of the darkness that lurked within him, the twisted ambition that drove him.

"Still as stubborn as ever, I see," he murmured, his tone laced with sarcasm, though there was a faint, chilling amusement in his gaze, a hint of satisfaction as he looked at Nolan, as though savoring the moment, relishing in the control he still held.

Nolan felt a surge of anger, a fierce, unyielding rage that cut through his fear, grounding him, filling him with a sense of purpose, a reminder of everything he'd fought to protect, everything he'd sacrificed to escape the shadow of this man.

But before he could speak, before he could let the words that burned within him spill out, Lucifer's gaze flicked to Rebecca, his smile widening, a faint, mocking glint in his eyes as he looked at her, as though appraising her, measuring her, a predator sizing up its prey.

"And who is this?" he murmured, his voice filled with a quiet, mocking amusement that sent a chill down Rebecca's spine, a reminder of the danger, the twisted ambition that lurked within him.

Rebecca held her ground, her gaze steady, though there was a faint tremor in her hands, a quiet, unspoken fear that she quickly masked with a look of fierce, unyielding determination. "Someone who's not interested in your games," she replied, her voice calm, steady, though there was a faint edge of defiance in her tone, a reminder that she wouldn't be intimidated, wouldn't be broken.

Lucifer's smile widened, his gaze flicking back to Nolan, a faint, mocking glint in his eyes. "She's got spirit," he murmured, his voice filled with a quiet, mocking admiration. "I can see why you'd keep her around. You always did have a taste for... the unusual."

Nolan felt a surge of anger, a fierce, protective instinct that cut through his fear, grounding him, filling him with a sense of purpose, a reminder of everything he'd fought to protect, everything he'd sacrificed to escape the shadow of this man.

"Leave her out of this," he growled, his voice low, filled with a quiet, restrained fury that cut through the silence, grounding him, steadying him.

Lucifer chuckled, a dark, hollow sound that echoed through the hallway, filling the air with a sense of unease, a reminder of the darkness that lurked within him, the twisted ambition that drove him.

"Oh, Nolan," he murmured, his tone laced with sarcasm, though there was a faint, chilling amusement in his gaze, a hint of satisfaction as he looked at Nolan, as though savoring the moment, relishing in the control he still held. "You always were so predictable."

Nolan clenched his fists, his gaze fixed on Lucifer, his mind racing, a storm of anger, fear, and something else—something raw and unyielding—swirling within him. But then he felt it—a quiet, gentle pressure against his hand, a touch that cut through his fear, grounding him, filling him with a sense of calm, a reminder that he wasn't alone.

He looked down, his gaze softening as he saw Rebecca's hand wrapped around his, her touch warm, steady, a silent promise that she was there, that she wouldn't leave him, that she would face this darkness with him, whatever the cost.

For a moment, they stood in silence, their gazes locked, a quiet, unspoken understanding passing between them, a bond that went beyond words, beyond fear, a connection that was as fragile as it was unbreakable.

Lucifer watched them, his gaze narrowing, his expression darkening as he took in the silent exchange, the quiet, unspoken connection that lingered in the air between them.

"Ah," he murmured, his tone filled with a faint, mocking amusement. "So that's how it is. Tell me, Nolan, does she know who you really are? What you've done?"

Rebecca felt a surge of anger, a fierce, protective instinct that cut through her fear, grounding her, filling her with a sense of purpose, a reminder of everything they'd fought for, everything they'd sacrificed to protect.

"He's a better man than you'll ever be," she replied, her voice calm, steady, though there was a faint edge of defiance in her tone, a reminder that she wouldn't be intimidated, wouldn't be broken.

Lucifer's smile widened, a faint, mocking glint in his eyes as he looked at her, as though savoring her defiance, relishing in the challenge she presented.

"We'll see," he murmured, his tone filled with a quiet, chilling promise that sent a shiver down her spine, a reminder of the darkness, the twisted ambition that drove him.

Nolan tightened his grip on her hand, his gaze fixed on Lucifer, his expression hard, unyielding, a fierce determination etched into every line of his face.

"We're leaving," he said, his voice low, filled with a quiet, restrained fury that cut through the silence, grounding him, steadying him.

Lucifer chuckled, a dark, hollow sound that echoed through the hallway, filling the air with a sense of unease, a reminder of the danger, the twisted ambition that lurked within him.

"Oh, I don't think so," he murmured, his tone laced with sarcasm, though there was a faint, chilling amusement in his gaze, a hint of satisfaction as he looked at Nolan, as though savoring the moment, relishing in the control he still held.

But then, in a swift, calculated movement, Nolan pulled Rebecca with him, his grip firm, steady, a fierce, unyielding strength that cut through her fear, grounding her, filling her with a sense of safety, a reminder that she wasn't alone.

They moved through the hallway, their steps quick, cautious, their senses honed to every flicker of movement, every distant echo of footsteps. Behind them, Lucifer's laughter echoed through the darkness, a hollow, chilling sound that sent a shiver down her spine, a reminder of the danger, the twisted ambition that lurked within him.

As they reached the exit, Rebecca looked up at Nolan, her gaze filled with a mixture of relief and something deeper, a quiet, unspoken attachment that lingered in the silence between them, a bond that went beyond words, beyond fear, a connection that was as fragile as it was unbreakable.

"Thank you," she murmured, her voice barely more than a whisper, though there was a faint, aching sincerity in her tone, a quiet, unspoken gratitude that cut through the tension, grounding her, steadying her.

He looked down at her, his gaze softening, his voice filled with a quiet, restrained protectiveness that left her breathless. "You don't need to thank me," he muttered, his tone laced with sarcasm, though there was a faint, reluctant warmth in his gaze, a quiet, unspoken connection that lingered in the silence between them. "Just stay close. We're not out of this yet."

They moved through the darkness, their steps quick, cautious, their senses honed to every flicker of movement, every distant echo of footsteps. And in that moment, as they navigated the shadows, a quiet, unspoken understanding settled between them, a bond that went beyond words, beyond pain, a connection that was as fragile as it was unbreakable.

Chapter 29: "Face to Face with the Enemy"

The air was heavy with a quiet, tense anticipation as they stood together in the cold, darkened expanse just beyond Lucifer's stronghold, the distant hum of generators and the occasional flicker of floodlights the only signs of life within the camp. They were both silent, each lost in thought, in the weight of everything that had brought them here, of everything they were about to face.

Nolan looked down at the worn, scratched surface of his weapon, his fingers tracing the familiar grooves, the cold, reassuring weight grounding him, steadying him. He felt Rebecca's gaze on him, her quiet presence a steady, unspoken support that cut through the darkness, a reminder of the strength, the purpose that had driven him to this point.

After a long moment, he glanced up, meeting her gaze, his expression softened by a quiet, unspoken sincerity, a bond that went beyond words, beyond logic. "Rebecca," he murmured, his voice barely more than a whisper, though there was a fierce, unyielding determination in his tone. "I need you to know... I'll protect you. No matter what."

Her gaze softened, her lips curving into a faint, sad smile, though there was a warmth in her expression, a quiet, unspoken gratitude that cut through the tension, grounding her, steadying her. "I know," she replied, her voice filled with a quiet, aching sincerity, a reminder of everything they'd endured, of everything they'd lost. "But I don't want you to do this for me, Nolan. I want you to do this for us."

He let out a short, humorless laugh, though there was a faint, reluctant warmth in his gaze, a quiet, unspoken connection that lingered in the silence between them. "Well, that just sounds like a bonus."

They fell into silence, the weight of everything they'd left unsaid, of everything they were about to face settling over them like a heavy, suffocating shroud. She stepped closer, her hand reaching out, resting on his arm, her touch warm, steady, a silent promise that she would stand by him, that she wouldn't leave him to face this darkness alone.

"Nolan," she murmured, her voice barely more than a whisper, though there was a fierce, unyielding strength in her tone, a quiet, unspoken conviction that cut through her fear, grounding her, filling her with a sense of purpose. "Whatever happens... I'm here with you. We'll face this together."

He looked down at her, his gaze softening, his expression filled with a quiet, unspoken vulnerability that cut through his defenses, that left him raw, exposed, a reminder of everything he'd fought to protect, of everything he'd tried to bury, to forget. And in that moment, he felt a surge of gratitude, a fierce, unyielding attachment that went beyond logic, beyond pain, a connection that was as fragile as it was unbreakable.

For a long moment, they held each other's gaze, a quiet, unspoken understanding passing between them, a bond that went beyond words, beyond fear, a connection that was as fierce as it was fragile. And then, as if by some unspoken agreement, he reached out, pulling her into his arms, holding her close, his grip firm, steady, a silent promise that he wouldn't let go, that he wouldn't leave her, not now, not ever.

She rested her head against his shoulder, her arms wrapping around him, her touch warm, grounding, a silent promise that she would stand by him, that she wouldn't leave him to face this darkness alone. They stayed like that for a long moment, the quiet, steady rhythm of their breaths filling the air, a reminder of the connection, the bond that had brought them here, that had kept them going, even in the face of impossible odds.

As they pulled back, their gazes locked, a quiet, unspoken understanding passing between them, a reminder of everything they'd left unsaid, of everything they were about to face. And in that moment, they both knew, deep down, that whatever happened, whatever dangers they faced, they would face it together, bound by a bond that was as fierce as it was unbreakable.

But then, just as they turned to face the camp, the distant sound of footsteps echoed through the darkness, a reminder of the dangers that lurked within, of the enemy that waited, that watched, a predator lurking in the shadows.

Nolan's grip on his weapon tightened, his posture tensing as he scanned the shadows, his senses honed to every flicker of movement, every distant echo, every reminder of the battle that lay ahead. He felt a cold, unyielding resolve settle over him, a fierce, unrelenting determination that cut through his fear, grounding him, filling him with a sense of purpose.

And then, as if summoned by his resolve, the shadows shifted, and Lucifer emerged, his figure silhouetted against the flickering light, his gaze fixed on them with a mixture of amusement and something darker, something twisted, a reminder of the ambition, the cruelty that had driven him, that had brought them all to this point.

"Well," he murmured, his voice smooth, mocking, filled with a quiet, deadly amusement. "It seems you've decided to make this interesting."

Nolan felt a surge of anger, a fierce, protective instinct that cut through his fear, grounding him, filling him with a sense of purpose, a reminder of everything he'd fought to protect, of everything he'd sacrificed to escape the shadow of this man.

"Interesting doesn't begin to cover it," he replied, his voice low, edged with a quiet, restrained fury that cut through the silence, grounding him, steadying him. "This ends here, Lucifer."

Lucifer chuckled, a dark, hollow sound that echoed through the darkness, filling the air with a sense of unease, a reminder of the danger, the twisted ambition that lurked within him. "Oh, I don't think so," he murmured, his tone laced with sarcasm, though there was a faint, chilling amusement in his gaze, a hint of satisfaction as he looked at them, as though savoring the moment, relishing in the control he still held.

Rebecca felt a surge of fear, a fierce, protective instinct that cut through her hesitation, grounding her, filling her with a sense of purpose, a reminder of everything they'd fought for, everything they'd sacrificed to protect. She reached for Nolan's hand, her fingers intertwining with his, a silent promise that she wouldn't leave him, that she would face this darkness with him, whatever the cost.

Nolan looked down at her, his gaze softening, his expression filled with a quiet, unspoken vulnerability that cut through his defenses, that left him raw, exposed, a reminder of everything he'd fought to protect, of everything he'd tried to bury, to forget. And in that moment, he felt a surge of gratitude, a fierce, unyielding attachment that went beyond logic, beyond pain, a connection that was as fragile as it was unbreakable.

"Let's do this," he murmured, his voice barely more than a whisper, though there was a fierce, unyielding determination in his tone, a reminder of the bond, the connection that had brought them here, that had kept them going, even in the face of impossible odds.

Rebecca squeezed his hand, her gaze steady, filled with a quiet, unspoken strength, a reminder of the fierce, unyielding bond that held them together, that had driven them to this point. "Together," she replied, her voice barely more than a whisper, though there was a fierce, unwavering conviction in her tone, a reminder of the connection, the bond that went beyond words, beyond fear.

They turned to face Lucifer, their postures tense, their gazes locked, a fierce, unyielding determination etched into every line of their bodies, a silent promise that they wouldn't back down, that they would face this darkness together, whatever the cost.

And as Lucifer's laughter echoed through the darkness, a hollow, chilling sound that filled the air with a sense of unease, they felt a surge of resolve, a fierce, unrelenting determination that cut through their fear, grounding them, steadying them, a reminder that they weren't alone, that they would face this battle side by side, bound by a bond that was as fierce as it was unbreakable.

In the silence that followed, they shared one last look, a quiet, unspoken understanding passing between them, a reminder of everything they'd left unsaid, of everything they were about to face. And in that moment, they both knew, deep down, that whatever happened, whatever dangers they faced, they would face it together, bound by a bond that was as fierce as it was fragile, a connection that went beyond words, beyond pain, beyond the unrelenting chaos that surrounded them.

The final battle awaited.

Chapter 30: "The Flame of Hope"

The morning sky was an angry swirl of crimson and deep blue as the first light crept over the mountains, casting long shadows across the smoldering ruins of Lucifer's fortress. The air was thick with the smell of smoke and iron, the remnants of past skirmishes littering the ground. Somewhere in the distance, a twisted metal gate creaked in the wind, the only sound in an otherwise oppressive silence.

Nolan adjusted his grip on his weapon, his knuckles white, his face a hard mask of concentration and tension. Beside him, Rebecca stood tall, the last traces of doubt stripped away, replaced by a quiet, fierce resolve. They were bruised, battered, but unyielding, their breaths mingling in the cold air, their hearts pounding with a single purpose: this was where it ended.

A faint, mocking laugh echoed from the shadows, followed by the slow, deliberate sound of footsteps. Lucifer emerged, his dark coat billowing behind him, his gaze cold, unfeeling, a twisted satisfaction glinting in his eyes as he looked at them.

"Well, well," he drawled, his voice a low, dangerous murmur. "I have to admit, I didn't think you'd make it this far."

Nolan met his gaze, his expression a mixture of defiance and disgust. "That's because you never understood what you were up against."

Lucifer chuckled, a hollow, humorless sound. "And what's that, Nolan? A ragtag duo armed with a misplaced sense of justice?"

Nolan's jaw clenched, but before he could respond, Rebecca stepped forward, her voice calm, steady, cutting through the tension. "No. We're armed with something you'll never understand."

Lucifer raised an eyebrow, a mocking smile playing at his lips. "And what might that be?"

"Hope," she replied, her gaze steady, unwavering. "Hope, and the will to do what you could never have the courage for."

Lucifer's smile faltered for a fraction of a second, his gaze narrowing, the faintest flicker of something unreadable flashing across his face before it was replaced by a cold, calculating gleam.

"Touching," he murmured, his tone dripping with sarcasm. "But I think you'll find hope is a fragile thing. Easily crushed."

Nolan's fingers tightened around his weapon, his gaze fixed on Lucifer with a fierce, unyielding determination. "So let's test that theory."

And then, with a shout, the final battle erupted.

Lucifer's forces descended upon them in a wave, dark figures emerging from the shadows, their eyes glinting with a dangerous, unfeeling light, their movements swift, calculated, honed for destruction. Nolan and Rebecca moved in unison, each movement precise, instinctive, as they fought side by side, a silent understanding passing between them, a bond forged in the heat of battle, unbreakable and unyielding.

Rebecca was a blur of movement, her every strike filled with a fierce, unyielding resolve, a reminder of the lives she was fighting for, the hope she carried within her, a flame that refused to be extinguished. Beside her, Nolan moved with a deadly efficiency, his every strike a calculated blow, a reminder of the determination that had driven him, the purpose that had kept him going, even in the face of impossible odds.

The battle was a cacophony of chaos and destruction, a symphony of clashing steel and shouted commands, each moment filled with the raw, unrelenting force of survival. And through it all, they fought with a fierce, unyielding resolve, a reminder of the bond that held them nection that had brought them here, that had kept ... when everything seemed lost.

As the battle raged on, Nolan caught sight of Lucifer, standing at the edge of the fray, his gaze fixed on them with a cold, calculating gleam, a twisted satisfaction glinting in his eyes as he watched his forces close in around them.

Nolan's gaze narrowed, a fierce, unyielding rage burning within him as he locked eyes with Lucifer, his voice low, steady, filled with a quiet, deadly promise. "This is for everyone you've taken, everything you've destroyed."

With a surge of adrenaline, he broke through the line of guards, charging toward Lucifer, his every step filled with a fierce, unrelenting determination, a reminder of the lives he was fighting for, the hope that had driven him, even in the face of impossible odds.

Lucifer met him with a cruel smile, his gaze filled with a twisted amusement as he raised his weapon, his movements swift, calculated, filled with the cold, unfeeling precision of someone who had spent years honing his craft, perfecting the art of destruction.

They clashed with a fierce, unyielding intensity, each strike a deadly dance, a battle of wills, a test of resolve, as they fought for control, for survival, for the lives that hung in the balance. And as the fight wore on, as the weight of exhaustion began to take its toll, Nolan felt a surge of strength, a fierce, unyielding resolve that cut through his fear, grounding him, filling him with a sense of purpose.

He thought of Rebecca, of the hope she had given him, the strength she had shown, the quiet, fierce resolve that had carried them both through the darkness, that had kept them going, even when everything seemed lost. And with one final surge of strength, he struck, his blow landing with a fierce, unrelenting force that sent Lucifer staggering back, his weapon clattering to the ground.

Lucifer fell to his knees, his gaze filled with a mixture of disbelief and fury, his face pale, a faint, twisted smile playing at his lips as he looked up at them, a reminder of the darkness that had driven him, th.. had brought them all to this point.

"Well done," he murmured, his voice filled with a faint, mocking amusement. "But I think you'll find that victory is a fleeting thing."

Nolan met his gaze, his expression hard, unyielding, a fierce, unrelenting determination etched into every line of his face. "Not this time."

With that, he turned, leaving Lucifer to the shadows, to the destruction he had wrought, to the legacy of chaos and despair that would be his only mark on the world.

Rebecca was at his side in an instant, her gaze filled with a mixture of relief and something deeper, a quiet, unspoken attachment that cut through the tension, grounding them, steadying them, a reminder of everything they had fought for, of everything they had endured, of the bond that had held them together, that had kept them going, even in the face of impossible odds.

They moved through the remnants of the battlefield, the quiet, heavy silence a stark contrast to the chaos that had filled the air moments before, a reminder of the cost, the price they had paid, the lives that had been lost.

As they reached the edge of the camp, Nolan turned to her, his expression softened by a quiet, unspoken gratitude, a silent acknowledgment of everything she had given him, of the hope she had rekindled within him, a reminder of the connection, the bond that had brought them here, that had kept them going.

"Rebecca," he murmured, his voice barely more than a whisper, though there was a fierce, unyielding sincerity in his tone. "I don't think I'd have made it without you."

She looked up at him, her gaze softened by a quiet, unspoken affection, a reminder of the bond that had held them together, that had carried them through the darkness, even when everything seemed lost.

"I'd say the same," she replied, her voice filled with a quiet, aching sincerity, though there was a faint, teasing warmth in her tone. "But I think you know that already."

They fell into silence, the weight of everything they'd endured, of everything they'd lost, settling over them like a heavy, suffocating shroud. But in that moment, as they stood together, side by side, a quiet, unspoken understanding passing between them, a bond that went beyond words, beyond pain, beyond the chaos that had surrounded them, they both knew, deep down, that they had found something worth fighting for, something worth holding on to.

Rebecca reached out, her hand finding his, her touch warm, grounding, a silent promise that she would stand by him, that she would face the future with him, whatever it held.

"Are you ready?" she murmured, her voice barely more than a whisper, though there was a faint, hopeful glimmer in her eyes, a reminder of the flame that had driven them, that had carried them through the darkness.

He looked down at her, his gaze softened by a quiet, unspoken affection, a reminder of the bond that had held them together, that had carried them through the chaos, even when everything seemed lost.

"With you? Yeah, I am."

They shared a quiet, tender smile, a silent acknowledgment of the future that awaited them, of the hope that had been rekindled, a reminder of the strength, the resilience that had carried them through, that would carry them forward, whatever the future held.

And as they turned to face the rising sun, a quiet, unspoken sense of hope settled over them, a reminder that, even in the darkest of times, there was always a light, a flame that refused to be extinguished.

Epilogue

The morning sun poured through the high windows of the makeshift clinic, casting long beams of light across rows of metal cots, neatly lined up in the dusty silence. Outside, the sound of muted voices rose and fell, the faint hum of conversation carrying on the cool morning breeze. It was a symphony of slow, careful hope—a tone Rebecca thought she might never hear again.

She moved through the rows, checking on the people who lay wrapped in clean white sheets, some sleeping, some talking quietly with family members, all resting under the faint glow of hope. It was strange, she thought, how this new world felt more fragile than ever, as though it could be lost at any moment if she let herself blink too long.

At the far end of the room, Nolan leaned against the wall, arms crossed, watching her with a faint smirk tugging at the corners of his mouth. His presence was steady, grounding, a reminder of the bond they shared, forged in fire and chaos and strengthened by everything they'd endured.

"Enjoying the view?" she asked, raising an eyebrow as she met his gaze, her tone light, laced with just a hint of sarcasm.

He shrugged, his smirk widening. "Just making sure you don't start getting ideas about going soft now that we've got clean sheets and fresh bandages. I'd hate to see you ruin your tough reputation."

She rolled her eyes, though there was a faint, reluctant smile playing at her lips. "Oh, please. If anyone's in danger of going soft, it's you. I caught you actually smiling at someone earlier."

Nolan feigned a look of horror, his voice a low, mocking drawl. "Don't spread that around. I've got an image to maintain, you know."

Rebecca shook her head, her smile softening as she looked at him, her gaze filled with a quiet, unspoken gratitude, a reminder of everything they'd fought for, everything they'd sacrificed. "Well, you're doing a terrible job of it."

They fell into silence, the weight of everything they'd endured, everything they'd lost settling over them like a heavy, suffocating shroud. She reached out, her hand finding his, her touch warm, grounding, a silent promise that she would stand by him, that she wouldn't leave him to face this darkness alone.

"Nolan," she murmured, her voice barely more than a whisper, though there was a fierce, unyielding strength in her tone, a quiet, unspoken conviction that cut through her fear, grounding her, filling her with a sense of purpose.

The quiet murmurs of the recovering patients and the smell of antiseptic drifted around them, mingling with the morning light filtering through the high windows. Outside, the world was tentatively stirring, starting to rebuild, but inside, the stillness carried a gravity—an acknowledgment of everything it had taken to get here.

Nolan leaned against the wall with an air of casual indifference that didn't fool Rebecca one bit. She could feel his eyes on her, assessing, making sure she hadn't gone too far in her rounds that morning. She moved between patients, her hands light as she checked bandages and pulses, her expression softening when she saw even a flicker of progress.

At last, she straightened, stretching out the ache in her back, and crossed over to him. His gaze was steady, sharp as always, but softened now by the faintest hint of warmth, a quiet attachment he rarely allowed himself to show.

"Done babysitting?" he asked, one eyebrow raised, his smirk barely contained.

She huffed a laugh, giving him a playful shove on the arm. "It's called 'healing,' Nolan. You could try it sometime."

He tilted his head, feigning deep thought. "And here I thought we were just giving the world a head start before it collapses all over again."

Rebecca crossed her arms, meeting his gaze with a challenging spark in her eyes. "And yet, here you are, very determined to make sure these people get that head start."

"Let's just say I've gotten used to certain... inconveniences," he muttered, looking away, his tone laced with sarcasm. But he didn't pull his hand from hers. Instead, his fingers tightened around hers, a subtle yet fierce reminder of the shared battles, the quiet strength they'd found in each other.

They moved together down the hall, side by side, and paused near the large windows at the far end of the clinic. Outside, the world stretched out, raw and wounded, yet carrying the first hints of green returning to the blackened earth. It was beautiful in a jagged, defiant way, and it was enough to bring a faint smile to her lips.

"So, what now?" she asked quietly, glancing over at him.

He met her gaze, his expression softened by a rare vulnerability, his voice low, threaded with a rough sincerity. "Now? Now we make sure this wasn't for nothing."

A pause stretched between them, filled with all the unspoken promises, the fragile hope that had carried them through so many dark nights. And then, before she could stop herself, she leaned into him, her head resting against his shoulder, her hand slipping into his.

For a long moment, they stood like that, surrounded by the soft sounds of the clinic, their shared silence a testament to the bond that had brought them here, to the strength they'd found in each other.

"Nolan," she whispered, her voice barely more than a breath, but filled with a quiet, unbreakable conviction. "Whatever happens... I'm with you."

He looked down at her, his gaze filled with a fierce, unyielding affection, a reminder of the battles they'd fought, the hope they'd refused to abandon. He didn't need to say it; she could see it in his eyes, the promise he'd made, the commitment he'd never let go.

"Good," he murmured, his tone laced with a faint, dry humor, a quiet acknowledgment of everything they'd endured. "Because I'd hate to go soft without you around to keep me in line."

She let out a soft laugh, her smile widening as she squeezed his hand, their fingers entwined, a silent promise of everything that lay ahead, of the hope that had carried them through, even when all seemed lost.

And as the first light of dawn spilled over the horizon, casting a warm, golden glow over the clinic, they stood together, a quiet, unbreakable bond between them, a reminder that, even in the darkest of times, there was always a flame of hope waiting to be rekindled.

Don't miss out!

Visit the website below and you can sign up to receive emails whenever Maximilian Krieg publishes a new book. There's no charge and no obligation.

https://books2read.com/r/B-A-IPGPC-KJEEF

BOOKS 2 READ

Connecting independent readers to independent writers.

Also by Maximilian Krieg

Waves of Chaos
Sunken Secrets: A Post-Apocalyptic Thriller of Survival and Deception in a Flooded World

Standalone
Die Maske der Lüge
Jenseits des Schattens: Ein okkulter Thriller
Love in the Time of Plague

About the Author

A former journalist turned thriller novelist, Maximilian Krieg combines his real-world experiences in war zones with a passion for high-stakes storytelling. Born in Munich, he draws inspiration from the darkest parts of human nature and the resilience of the human spirit. His books are known for their gritty realism and complex characters.